Gone

But

Loved Forever

Sandra Kinslow and her Grandfather Chet Newton

By

Sandra Kinslow

Dedication

My Grandpa Chet Newton-Hector, Ark

Author: Sandra Kinslow & Chet Newton

My grandfather always encouraged me to use my God-given
talent to create stories. He was known as a great storyteller, and
everyone enjoyed his shared stories.

My grandfather was my inspiration when I was writing this
book.

About the Author

Books Published by Author Sandra Kinslow

- — Lost in A Dark Forest
- — Stalker Lurking in the Shadows
- — The Shadows of Jennifer
- — A Life Lost but Not Forgotten
- — Run Stubby Run

Contents

CHAPTER 1

Not Forgotten

Waking up from a night of restless sleep, Jennifer lay there for a few moments. She knew Davie would be returning home today. He was out of town doing some investigative work for the police department. She missed him when he was gone, even if it was just for a few days.

Davie's mom had called yesterday. She thought we might enjoy some time together without the kids and asked if she could come to get the grandkids for a few days. Jennifer had told her the kids could spend the weekend. She knew the kids would enjoy the time with their grandparents.

She took a shower and later decided to change the sheets on the bed and hang them outside on the clothesline. She usually put them in the dryer, but the breeze blowing out would dry the sheets quickly.

Hearing the washing machine stop, Jennifer grabbed her basket, took the sheets, and hung them on the clothesline.

Sitting in her favorite rocking chair on the porch, she took a sip of coffee and then sat back in the chair.

Shutting her eyes, she listened to the sounds of the birds and the water rippling in the lake near the house.

Hearing a car coming up their driveway, she opened her eyes to see who was coming to their house. It was too early for Davie to be back home.

It was a beautiful red Corvette, and the young man who got out of the car was tall with blonde hair and glasses. She could not imagine who he might be because she did not recognize the car or him.

Standing up, she waited for him to come to the porch. She thought he might need help locating someone. When he got to the porch, she panicked when she realized who was standing before her.

The young man took off his sunglasses. The blonde hair had fooled her. When he took off his sunglasses, she knew who had come to her house.

She turned to go inside so that she could lock the door, but he grabbed her before she could get the storm door open. She reached for her cell phone, but it was not there. She had left it lying on the table in the kitchen.

Jennifer had filed a report with the police several years ago regarding his attempt to rape her. After getting a warrant for his arrest, the police put him in jail. He had to appear before the Judge, so his trial date could be set for the attempted rape charge.

Looking straight at her, Rick told her in handcuffs when he left the courthouse that day, "I will be back someday and get what I wanted from you." Rick disappeared before his trial date.

Seeing him standing there now, with a death grip on her, she knew exactly why he was back. She had struggled the first time he had tried to force her to have sex with him. She had refused him sex. Now he was back and still trying to get what he wanted.

If a stranger had not come down the road that night and seen what the man was trying to do to her, Rick would have raped her that night. Now he was back and standing on her porch with that same look in his eyes he had when he had tried to force her to have sex with him several years ago.

After grabbing her by the wrist, he dragged her through the house to their bedroom.

Jennifer begged him not to do this to her and to leave. She resisted and struggled to escape him, but he slapped her and told her to shut up.

He threw her on the bed. He forced himself on her despite her screams. He continued to abuse her sexually. Jennifer was pregnant and feared for the baby she was carrying because of the disgusting, painful, brutal things he was doing to her.

Screaming out in pain and disgust only made him slap her again. He wasted no time getting what he came for, and then he hit her so hard she lost consciousness.

When she came to, what she feared was happening. She knew she was having a miscarriage. She knew she had to get help because she was having a miscarriage and losing her precious baby girl. She left the bed and tried to get to her phone in the kitchen. She passed out again on the way to the kitchen.

Rick was laughing when he left Jennifer's house. He was proud to show her he always got what he wanted. He did not allow his dates to get away by saying "No" to him. He had tried to get what he wanted on the last date with Jennifer.

She had told him that night it was over between them and had resisted him, but "Rick did not like her resisting him and saying "No" to him.

Rick did not know who the stranger was that night, who had stopped his car and drug him off, Jennifer. This man hit him so hard that he never knew what happened before he had a chance to get what he wanted that night from Jennifer, "sex." She had always pushed him away but had no one to rescue her this time. He finally got what he had wanted from her this time.

Leaving the house, he took off in his Corvette. He knew he needed to escape the town quickly before Jennifer regained consciousness and called the police.

Rick decided to go back to where their home was in Rosewood. He needed to shower, change his clothes, and leave town quickly. He had flown there in his mom's jet but decided not to use it on the return trip. He would fly back on a commercial flight.

He spotted a police car at the stop sign. He knew he had fled the country after he had appeared in court for his attempted rape, so he took off easy from the stop sign to keep from drawing attention to his car.

When he arrived at his home in Rosewood, he used the garage remote outside the garage and let himself into the house.

After a shower and changing some of his clothes hanging in the closet, he left for the airport. He had called the airport and made reservations for a flight that would go in an hour.

Rick found in his bedroom a passport he had used in the past, which had his picture and a different name. He also had a recent driver's license, with that same name and blonde hair. He took those things with him.

His parents did not know he had a different driver's license and passport. He used this ID when he did not want his parents to know where he had gone.

Rick left his red Corvette rental car at the airport and checked in at the airport for his flight to Europe.

He took a commercial flight back to Europe instead of their private jet as planned. His mom and dad would be furious if they knew he had gone to see Jennifer. They thought he was just traveling some for the fun of it.

Davie headed home and thought he would call Jennifer and tell her he would be home soon. He was surprised when she never answered her cell phone. She never went anywhere without her phone.

He tried again to reach her, and no answer. He was getting concerned. He knew the kids were at his parents' house. Using his phone, he called the precinct and asked them if they had a patrol car near his house.

He told them, "Jennifer is not answering her phone, and it will be fifteen minutes before I get home. Jennifer is having problems with this pregnancy, and I am worried about her."

They told him they had a car in the area. They would drive over to his house and make sure she was okay.

Davie turned on his blue lights and headed home. He had a feeling something was wrong.

The officer arrived at Davie's house, and everything seemed okay. He noticed sheets were hanging on the line, and a cup of coffee was sitting on the table on the porch.

Approaching the house, the officer knocked and called out to Jennifer. She did not answer when he called her name. The main door was open. He opened the storm door and called out to her to let her know the police were there.

Walking into the kitchen, he saw her lying unconscious between the cabinet and the island. Her phone was lying on the island. She must have tried to get to her phone but passed out before she could call for help.

The officer called Davie to let him know he was there at his home. He told Davie, "I also called for an ambulance because I found Jennifer unconscious. I also called for backup because I saw bruises on her face and arms, and she was bleeding like she might be having a miscarriage."

When the ambulance arrived, they examined Jennifer and determined she was losing the baby.

Their examination at the hospital revealed she had been raped, beaten brutally, and physically attacked by the rapist and was at risk of a miscarriage.

The doctor took her to surgery to do a C-section in hopes of being able to save the baby. Whatever she had been through was too much trauma for the baby, and the doctors could not keep the baby.

When Davie arrived at the hospital, the doctor said, "Jennifer is not okay. We did a C-section to try to save the baby. The baby could not be saved due to the trauma from the rape. She will need to stay in the hospital for a while.

We will watch Jennifer closely, and the nurse will let you know when you can go back to see her in the ICU. We were concerned about her being unconscious and in rough shape when the ambulance brought her to the hospital. They hoped she would wake up soon."

Davie called his mom and dad, saying, "I am at the hospital because Jennifer had a miscarriage. She is still unconscious, and I will call you later."

The officer who had called Davie arrived at the hospital. He filled Davie in on what he saw at the house. He also said he was concerned about bruises on her arms and face.

He said, "Davie, we will continue to check for clues about what happened at the house. The most important thing right now is you being here to care for Jennifer. We know how much you two love each other.

Davie had been so excited knowing Jennifer was having another baby.

When Jennifer had twins, she also suffered from severe medical problems after giving birth to twins. Several years passed, with her believing she would never be able to have any more children, but she was pregnant with this baby. Now Jennifer had lost this baby because of the cruelty of this rapist.

Davie was upset and wanted to see Jennifer. He wished he had never gone out of town. He was so heartbroken for her and the loss of their baby. He knew she would be devastated when she woke up and knew she had lost their baby.

The nurse came out and told Davie, "We will let you know when you see her. Right now, she is having breathing problems and is still unconscious."

Jennifer's mom and dad arrived at the hospital. They were also upset that she had lost the baby and concerned about why Jennifer was not waking up.

Davie told them, "The police thought someone had come to the house and had been brutal to Jennifer.

The doctor told me his examination revealed Jennifer had been physically abused, and she had been sexually abused. She appeared to have struggled and tried to free herself. Due to the brutality of being sexually abused, she was losing her baby.

The surgeon tried to save the baby, but the trauma was too much for the baby. He also said the trauma from the abuse had caused her to lose her baby.

The doctor said, "Be prepared to see Jennifer's face swollen. The bruises are also starting to surface on her face and arms. He also said Jennifer was unconscious when they brought her to the hospital and is still unconscious. He was concerned about being unable to arouse or wake her up after surgery."

They were all upset that someone would be so brutal to their precious Jennifer. Jennifer had been through so much, and now this.

Peggy and Tom sat there in the waiting room with Davie. You could see the pain on his face and how upset and angry he was that someone had done this to his sweet, beautiful wife.

Peggy did not blame him for being so upset because she was angry, and so was Tom that someone would be so cruel to Jennifer.

They were finally able to see Jennifer in the ICU. She looked so lifeless lying there in the bed. She was so pale, her face swollen, and bruises on her face and arms. The nurses had been unable to get her awake.

Davie spoke to her, but there was no response.

Peggy remembered how hard it was for Jennifer when that boyfriend she had dated in High School tried to sexually attack her one night when Jennifer had told him it was over between them.

She had broken up with him because he would not take "No" for an answer. He would try to get too fresh with her.

It had taken a year of therapy to put that attempt behind her.

It troubled Peggy to see her daughter in the ICU after someone had violated her and caused her to lose the baby.

Visitation time was over, so they left her room. They returned to the waiting room. Tom and Peggy found a quiet spot and prayed for their daughter and Davie.

Davie was pacing the floor, and the more he paced, the more upset he got.

He called the police station and asked them to make sure they had all the evidence they needed to support a case that involved the forceful assault of his wife, which had cost her to lose the baby.

They assured him they were still checking for leads, had gone over the whole house, and had some fingerprints on a few things, like the door casing on the porch.

Jennifer stayed in this stupor of sleep for several weeks. She seemed unable to wake up and cope with all that happened. When she finally woke up, she started crying and sobbing so hard that the doctor had to give her something to calm her down.

When Jennifer finally woke up again, she refused the food they offered her. She seemed afraid and did not want to talk to anyone or touch her. She cried a lot and then drifted back to sleep.

The doctors told Davie, "Your wife was lucky to have survived after she had been forcibly, brutally raped, and blessed to be alive. She will carry the scars of that for the rest of her life, both physically and emotionally, due to internal damage.

Davie was thankful Jennifer had survived and was still with them. He dropped his head and said a prayer for her.

Davie knew his wife was dealing with all of this and the loss of the baby. She had looked forward to giving birth to a baby girl. The whole family had been excited when she told them she was pregnant, and it was a little girl.

The hospital released her from the hospital after she gained consciousness and was able physically to go home. The doctor recommended therapy to help her deal with losing her baby.

After Jennifer left the hospital, Tom and Peggy decided to stay and take care of the children. They knew Jennifer would need rest, the adjustments in her life, and all that happened. This would not be easy. Peggy wanted to be nearby to help her daughter through this traumatic time in her life.

Jennifer spoke not a word on the trip home from the hospital. She got more restless as they got closer to the house. Davie was watching her and kept silent as he drove home. He could sense and feel her tense up by her body language.

Peggy and Tom were waiting on the porch when they arrived. She had made sure the house was clean, and Jennifer's bed was ready for her. Peggy did not know the sexual abuse had occurred in David and Jennifer's bedroom.

When Jennifer walked slowly into the house, she began to shake and cry. Jennifer turned and ran out of the house and out into the yard. She was back where he had raped her; the memories were too much to face now.

Davie took a few lawn chairs out where she was sitting on the ground.

He started to put his arms around her to help her up from the ground, but she panicked, jumped, and started walking down the driveway.

She could not stand someone touching her right now. She did not want the nurses and doctors touching her in the hospital, so they ensured no one touched her. Jennifer walked up and down the driveway two times. Walking was painful, and she was tired and turned back toward the house.

The walk had helped her realize she was in bad shape. Jennifer knew she needed help to deal with the death of her baby and did not want to talk about the rape.

A therapist helped her before when Rick attempted to get what he thought was his. When it was time to get help, she would call her therapist and make an appointment.

When she returned to the house, she walked up the sidewalk, opened the door, and walked inside. Davie was right behind her. He felt so helpless. He had stayed in the yard close by when she was outside, walking up and down the driveway.

How would he take care of her and offer his love and support if he could not touch her, and she refused to talk about what happened?

Jennifer sat down in a chair near the door. She wanted to leave and never return here but could not because this was their home.

She looked at Davie and saw the pain in his eyes and felt bad she was rejecting him or his hugs or offers to help.

She knew she needed help, but only getting through the night would be a huge challenge.

When her mom learned the rape had occurred in their bedroom. She shut the door to that bedroom.

She also cleaned the room well and prepared it for her and Davie to use later. She was not sure her daughter would ever be able to sleep in that room again.

When it got to bedtime, Davie knew that Jennifer would not want to sleep in their bed, knowing it was where this horrible thing happened to her.

Peggy helped Jennifer get ready for bed. Jennifer would not let her mom touch her but was glad she was nearby. Peggy helped Jennifer get prepared for bed. Jennifer would not let her mom touch her but was glad she was nearby. Peggy realized her daughter needed their love, support, and presence most.

Jennifer wanted to sleep on the couch, so her mom put some sheets and blankets on the couch.

The next morning, Davie and Tom ate breakfast at the table.

Her dad said little, but Davie knew how much he loved Jennifer. Tom was like him and troubled that someone would rape Jennifer and cause her to lose the baby.

Davie recalled helping Tom find Jennifer when the stalker had kidnapped her, and no one knew where he had taken her.

Tom had been a wonderful father to Jennifer. They both had been wonderful parents, and Jennifer missed them after they had moved to where they lived now.

Tom spoke to Davie and said, "I wish I could find the one who did this to my daughter.

He cost her the life of the baby she carried and took her away from us. I want to find him and tell him what I think of him."

Davie noticed Jennifer was waking up, so he told Tom, "We will talk later." Tom nodded, turned around, and saw Jennifer getting up from the couch where she had slept last night.

He said, "Yes, we can talk later; she is not going to want us to talk about it right now."

Jennifer had not slept much last night. She knew it would take her time to heal. Looking into the mirror, she saw how bruised she was. Then she remembered him slapping her so hard that she was dazed.

Looking away from the mirror, she dressed but was glad her mom was there with her, and she also realized she was not the only one hurting. Davie had lost the baby, too, and so had her family.

Davie needed to go to the police station to ensure they did everything required to find the one who did this to Jennifer. He would go to work with her mom and dad, and his parents were there to help.

His work would be good therapy because he felt helpless to do much for Jennifer now.

There had been no chance to grieve the loss of his unborn baby daughter.

After several days of being home and getting some rest, Jennifer wanted to see the kids. She was missing them. Jennifer did not realize she was unprepared for the hugs and kisses her kids always gave her.

Tom went to Marilyn's and Jerry's house to pick up the kids. Peggy did not want to leave Jennifer there by herself.

The kids were ready to go home, especially with Grandpa and Grandma Peggy there to visit them. Tom thanked Marilyn and Jerry for helping with the kids and knew they had received loving care while they were there. Marilyn and Jerry loved their grandkids.

Jimmy and Jenny knew their mom had lost the baby, and they were eager to see their mom.

They were sad, too, because they had looked forward to their sister being born.

They did not know about the rape but knew they were not getting a little sister now.

Jennifer was looking forward to the kids getting home. As soon as they walked through the door, they ran to her and crawled up in her lap, and

she screamed and pushed the kids away. It was painful for her, but she panicked when they touched her.

Peggy said, "Kids, your mom is sore, and she loves you, and we must be careful right now and save our hugs and kisses for later."

Both kids looked at their mom and said, "We are sorry, Mom, we did not know you were sore.

We see the bruises on your face, so we will save our hugs and kisses for later."

Peggy looked at Jennifer and said, "Tom and Jimmy can do some things together, and I think I will take Jenny to the kitchen with me, and we can make some cookies.

I thought you might want to get some more rest. Davie has gone to work to do some things but will return later."

Jennifer felt so bad; she screamed and pushed the kids away. What a terrible thing to do to her kids. She thanked her mom and said she would lie down on the couch.

Tom and Jimmy got the fishing pole and stuff and headed to the lake there near the house.

Peggy and Jenny made their way to the kitchen.

With tears in her eyes, Jennifer lay down on the couch. She started gently rubbing her tummy as she had done many times during her pregnancy and realized her baby was not there. She sobbed quietly into her pillow and finally drifted off to sleep.

Davie made some phone calls from his office at the station. Everyone there today had come to him and offered their help and sympathy.

He knew he had to keep it together and get things done despite his loss and his wife's terrible shape from all that happened.

Davie realized nothing had been done by the family about a service for the baby. He would talk to his parents, Tom and Peggy, about helping him make arrangements to bury the baby.

Davie knew Jennifer could not attend the services for the baby at this time. He would call and make the arrangements for burial.

They could have a special service later when she was able to attend.

He learned from the hospital that Jennifer never saw the baby due to being unconscious at that time.

Davie got to see his baby girl at the hospital and took pictures of their baby girl he could show Jennifer later. She was a beautiful baby girl like her mama.

After making several calls, he walked into his boss's office. He said, "I want to review all the evidence collected at the house. I like this man found, arrested, and brought to court.

I will approach this problem with an open mind despite my loss. I want to be at least able to help Jennifer put this behind her when we find this rapist, arrest him, and put him in jail.

I know Jennifer will need extended therapy. We will make sure she gets that as soon as she is physically able to get help. In the meantime, I may need time off. Jennifer's mom and dad will stay with us to help with the kids and her.

Jennifer is in bad shape and cannot stand even to be touched. I must be patient, loving, and caring however I can."

Captain Robert assured Davie that he would oversee the investigative work that needed to be done regarding this case.

He told Davie to take whatever time he needed from work to help at home.

Jennifer woke up and walked to the kitchen. Walking was painful, but she knew it would take her body, mind, and soul to adjust and heal.

Arriving in the kitchen, she saw a big smile on Jenny's face when they took the cookies out of the oven.

Jenny said, "Mom, can I bring you a cookie and some milk?"

Jennifer almost cried and knew it would be hard for her kids to see her like this.

She said, "Honey, I would love to have one of your cookies. Could you put it right over here on the table?"

Jenny said, "Sure, Mom, I will do that, and I love you, and when you feel like you are okay for a hug, you can let me know."

She laid the cookie on a paper towel, got her mom a glass of milk, and got one for her grandma and her. They sat around the island, eating their cookies.

Grandpa and Jimmy came in carrying the string of fish they had caught. Jimmy put the fish in the sink and told his grandma that when they finished their cookies and milk, they would take it outside and prepare it for frying.

Davie left the station to go home and see how things were at the house.

Tom met him in the driveway, reminding him of what happened when the kids got home. He told him how Jennifer had reacted regarding the kids.

He said, "We will stay and help for whatever time it takes for our daughter and be here for you and the kids."

Davie said, "Thanks to both of you for being here and helping with Jennifer and the kids. I know Jennifer needs you here right now, and so do I and the kids.

I also need your help, Tom; when we can investigate what happened here, I will need you here to help me.

Jimmy and Jenny saw their dad through the door and gave their dad big hugs and kisses. Jennifer watched them and knew she had missed wonderful times with her kids. It made her incredibly sad that she had so many problems adjusting and accepting what had happened. She also knew she was not physically able to get the kind of help she needed.

Davie approached Jennifer and said, "I see some cookies, and I bet my daughter helped make them. I would like to have some cookies too, and some milk.

Jennifer sat there and could not even move. She wanted to get up and get him some cookies, but she was numb and looked at him with sad and troubled eyes.

Jenny saw her mom looking sad and said, "Mom, you just sit there, and I will get Daddy his cookies and milk."

Jennifer looked at her precious little girl and was so proud of her.

Jenny said, "Mom, Dad, and I will be here to help you, and so will Jimmy, Grandpa, and Grandma. You just rest. We will help you and do whatever you need us to help you get well."

She kissed her mom and got her dad the milk and cookies.

Peggy had left the kitchen and went to the bathroom to cry. What a precious family, and how sad that it was to see her beloved daughter, whom she loved, in this condition.

CHAPTER 2

Changes Needed

Several weeks had passed since the doctor told him they could not save the baby. Davie knew something needed to be done regarding the baby and the services and burial for the baby.

Davie called the funeral home and told them about the baby and Jennifer's condition. He told them that any services for the baby would need to be done later. They said they would take care of things there so the baby could be buried later.

Peggy and Tom stayed and helped. Tom slept in the twin bed in Jimmy's room, and Peggy slept in Jenny's other twin bed in her room. Davie had brought in his camping cot and was sleeping on it. He was not getting much sleep at night. The cot made it possible for him to be close to Jennifer, who slept each night on the couch.

He had already realized their bedroom was not a good place for them at this time. It had too many bad memories for Jennifer, and she kept everyone at a distance and refused to talk about the rape. They sure needed to hear from her what happened, but it would have to wait until she could share it with them.

The police realized their limitations to what they could do to investigate since they had no clue who had done this to Jennifer. They needed a description of the rapist, and then they could try to locate him.

They knew she could help them find him, but she was still struggling to come to grips with everything and could not offer her help.

Davie stopped after work to pick up the mail in the mailbox at the end of their driveway. Their elderly neighbor came out to the mailbox, and she said, "Davie if you have a minute, I would like to talk to you. I hated hearing about what had happened to Jennifer, her losing the baby, and why she lost the baby.

Davie said, "Yes, ma'am, I have time."

She said, "Great because I do not know if what I am telling you will help you find whoever did this to your wife, but I saw a fancy car pull into your driveway that morning when she was raped. Not long before, that same car came back up the driveway and left in a big hurry. It was one of those fancy sports cars they call a Corvette or something like that. It was a red car.

I could not see the car's driver very well, but it looked like he had blonde hair. I do not know if this information will help you, but I know you are a good detective, and I thought this might help. It might be a while before Jennifer can talk about something that horrible."

Davie hugged her and said, "Bless your heart; you told me some things I would check out on my laptop. You have given me a clue to work with.

Thank you so much for being such wonderful neighbors for Uncle Joe and Aunt Bea when they were living here and neighbors for us."

Driving up the driveway, Davie remembered Jennifer telling him about Rick, a guy she had dated while he was still in the Army. He drove a red Corvette, and she said she broke up with him the night he tried to rape her.

Davie knew they had tried for several years to locate Rick but were unsuccessful. A special alert was sent by the police department to all the major police stations in hopes that they could help them find Rick.

They had also asked the FBI to assist them. According to the files, the FBI had no leads to help them find Rick but were still working on the case.

Rick's parents were rich and had a private jet. The police figured his mom had taken off with him in the jet right after she bailed him out of jail.

Davie wondered if there was a chance that Rick had sneaked back into the country and come back to keep the promise he had made to Jennifer when the police took him in handcuffs out of the courthouse. Davie thought it was worth opening Rick's case again.

Davie knew their neighbor had seen a red Corvette go down the driveway, and later, she saw him leave the driveway.

The police lost valuable time locating the man who had sexually abused Jennifer. Jennifer was full of anger. It frightened the kids when they saw their mom so full of anger, and they did not go near her.

Peggy noticed the change in the kids since Jennifer was home. Tom agreed with Peggy that Jennifer's emotional, angry fits of rage were scaring the kids. They were deeply concerned about how much this was affecting the grandkids.

Davie knew something needed to be done soon. She was physically getting stronger, but the sleeping arrangements were hard for them and Tom and Peggy.

He missed having her there in bed with him each night. He understood why she was sleeping on the couch at this time. The kids loved sharing their rooms with their grandparents but felt the changes that affected them.

Davie talked to Jennifer about selling the house and buying another one somewhere. When he told Jennifer this, she was furious and said, "No, I don't want another house; I just want the horrible experience to go away."

The only solution Davie could think of was to build them another room in the house. They could build a bedroom for them. Their old bedroom held so many bad memories for Jennifer. This room could be renovated and made a guest room for the grandparents or friends to use.

He talked to his mom and dad about building another room. His dad thought it was a great plan.

Jerry said, "Son, with my experience as a carpenter, I can greatly help. Tom is also a good carpenter with some experience. We can get some of the work done between us before the contractors come with their tools and finish the room for you."

When he got home from work, Davie told Tom he needed to talk to him.

They took lawn chairs down to the lake. Tom was eager to hear what Davie was going to tell him because he saw a smile on Davie's face for the first time since all of this had happened.

Davie said, "Tom, as you know, Jennifer is still struggling to understand what has happened. She is still sleeping on the couch and refuses to even go near that room we called our bedroom.

I asked Jennifer if it would help if we sold our place and moved elsewhere. She got pretty upset with me for even thinking about moving from here.

I was talking to dad today. I told him I was considering building a spacious room at the back of the house. We could build ourselves a master bedroom and a large bathroom. I hope building this room in our house would be good for Jennifer.

We can turn our old bedroom into a guest room for you, Peggy, and others who want to visit. I want the old room completely renovated.

Jerry and I are hopeful you will be free to help us. We want to do some work ourselves and let the contractors finish the room. I know you are a good carpenter, Tom.

Dad said he would help us, and we could do it faster. I told him I would talk to you and see if you would still be available and wanted to help.

I will be working during the day, so if you can help dad while I work, I can come home in the evenings and help."

Tom said, "That makes a lot of sense, and I would love to help you build that room. I think it would be wonderful therapy for Jennifer.

We will stay longer and help with the building and with the kids. I know it has been rough with the sleeping arrangements for you and Jennifer.

This has been a tough time for everyone. The grandkids do not seem to mind us sleeping with them, but a guest bedroom would be nice when we come to help with the kids or visit.

Peggy will be thrilled and can help Jennifer shop for the new room if she wants her to be a part of the shopping for things for the bedroom and bathroom.

I think you should build it big enough for a big bathroom for both of you.

I know that Peggy can help us renovate the old bedroom if Jennifer does not want to be a part of that job. This is the best news I have had and a chance to help you both through this period of adjustments.

Thanks for including us to help you with this. Not only will it help you not to have to pay for help, but you will get it built the way you want it with us helping you. I know Jerry is like me and works for nothing when it comes to helping the family."

Davie said, "We will share this news with the family tonight at the supper table and can start drawing up some plans. The sooner we start, the better.

I also have some news about something the little lady next door shared with me.

She said she had seen a red Corvette turn in our driveway the day Jennifer was raped. She knew I was gone but did not recognize that car. She saw that same car leaving a little later,   and it left in a hurry.

She wondered if the man in that car might be the one who did that horrible thing to Jennifer and caused her to lose their baby.

I hugged her and thanked her for the information. Now I have a lead, and I can start working on finding the one who molested my wife I love so much.

After I left our neighbor, I started thinking about something Jennifer shared about a boyfriend she dated when I was in the service that had tried to rape her. She said he drove a red Corvette."

Tom said, "Lois might have something there. Yes, Rick drove a red Corvette.

When he left the courthouse that day, he told Jennifer he would return some day because he always got what he wanted."

Davie said, "Yes, as soon as his mom paid the outrageous amount of bail money, we wondered if he would show up at the courthouse when it was time to return for the court hearing again. He was a no-show on the date he was supposed to be there.

A warrant was issued for his arrest for failing to appear in court.

We tried to find him, with help from other police precincts and some help from the FBI, but could not locate him.

I wonder if he might have sneaked back into the country if he lived in another country to ensure Jennifer knew he always got what he wanted."

Peggy had seen Jennifer in a bad state of mind after Rick had attempted to violate her when he dated her. She was also in a bad state of mind when the stalker stalked her, kidnapped her, and held her hostage.

Thankfully, they found a good therapist to help Jennifer at that time. Hopefully, Jennifer will also allow that therapist or someone qualified to help her this time.

Jennifer was not sleeping well and would still not let anyone touch her, not even the kids. She was restless and full of anger and fury. She paced the floors and was in bad shape regarding what had happened to her this time."

When Davie got home, he took something to drink out on the porch. Peggy joined him with a glass of tea. She expressed her concerns about her daughter's state of mind and how she was fearful she would hurt the kids during one of her rages of anger.

She said, "I think a good therapist like she had years ago would be helpful at this time for Jennifer.

Davie said, "Peggy, can you get me the name of this therapist?"

Peggy said, "Right now, I cannot recall the therapist's name, but I have it written down in my address book at home.

When we return to the house, I will get the name and phone number."

Jennifer woke up while her mom and Davie were talking. She heard what they said about her.

This troubled Jennifer is hearing how she hurt Jimmy Joe by pushing him back when he touched her. She lay on the couch in tears, knowing her actions hurt those she loved.

They were right; she needed some help. Somehow, some way, she had to get a grip on this and get help.

She felt so much pain from losing her baby and the horrible, vile rape. She wanted to escape from all this pain and how this made her feel.

Looking around the room, she knew Davie was willing to move away from there if that would help her; he had mentioned moving to her. She did not want to leave their home. There were lots of good memories of living here. It was a perfect place for them to raise the kids.

Walking out on the porch, Davie and Peggy could tell Jennifer had been crying.

She sat in the lawn chair near Davie. Looking at him, she could see he was suffering from their loss of the baby, and her treating him like she was doing it also hurt him.

It was up to her to find within herself what she needed to stop hiding in a shell and pushing everyone who loved her away from her. Her family loved her so much. She loved them and thanked God for each one of them.

Not saying a word, she kept looking into Davie's eyes and saw his love for her and his sadness.

Davie stood up, and Jennifer rose from her chair. She reached out to him with her arms extended toward him. He gently took her into his arms and held her in a loving, gentle, caring way. He whispered in her ear; with God's help, we will get through this together. I love you, Jennifer, and always will."

Jennifer started crying and said, "Davie, I love you too. I am so sorry I am in such a horrible state of mind and hurting the ones I love. I know I need help to put this behind me. So thankful for you and your love and the love of family."

Davie released her and said, "I am here for always, and we have so much to be thankful for. I want you to do whatever you need to enjoy your family and loved ones again."

Jennifer reached up and touched his cheek, and smiled. Davie knew, looking back into her eyes. With her touch, Jennifer was trying to find healing and recovery. He knew patience would help her to find the path back to them.

Jimmy hollered, "Dad, we want you to come here because we found the cutest turtle. We want you to see the turtle we found."

Jennifer took Davie's hand and said, "I want to see the turtle too."

He was thrilled and said, "Okay, we will see the turtle." Davie was happy to see her finally reaching out to him.

She dropped his hand when they reached the lake and stood before Jenny and Jimmy. She reached out to them. For a moment, they just stood there looking at her.

Jimmy got Jenny by the hand, and they reached out to their mom. She wrapped her arms around them. Tears filled her eyes as she held them close to her.

Jimmy said, "Mom, it is going to be okay. Dad and I will take care of you and Jenny."

With tears in his eyes, Davie embraced his children and wife. He knew with God's help, they would find a way to help Jennifer heal and gain her strength back.

Peggy joined them at the lake. She had tears in her eyes as she had witnessed her daughter finding within herself the strength and love for family, which helped her reach out to them with her love.

Jimmy Joe looked down at the turtle. He said, "Mom, I think the turtle likes you because he has crawled on top of your foot."

Jennifer reached down, picked up the turtle, and put it in Jimmy's hand. As he held the turtle, it crawled back inside its shell. She realized she had been hiding in a shell because of her pain.

The turtle finally stuck his head and feet out of his shell. Jennifer realized now what she had to do. No more ducking into her shell, hiding her pain, and keeping the people who loved her at a distance.

Bending over, she put out her hand to Jimmy. He let her hold his turtle. Holding the turtle, she thought, "I need to keep you around to remind me not to duck into a shell every time I feel pain or fear."

When they returned to the house, Jenny and Jimmy wanted to know if they could go home with Grandpa and Grandma Peggy for the weekend. Peggy nodded, and it was okay.

Davie looked at Jennifer, and she said, "Kids, I think that is a great idea, and your grandma has nodded; it is okay with them."

Jennifer was glad to have some time with Davie. She wanted to talk to Davie about some things that had happened.

Jennifer bent down to the kids and said, "Mommy will be okay. It might take me a little while to get well, but I will have the help I need from you and Dad.

I also have the love and help of your grandparents. You have an enjoyable time with your grandparents and God. I will see you Sunday night when you return."

The kids took off to their rooms to get the things they needed for the weekend.

Jennifer told mom, "I want you to find the phone number of the therapist I had when Rick tried to rape me back when I was dating him. I liked this therapist, and she helped me a lot."

The kids had their things together and were ready to go. They stopped and walked over to their mom and dad to say goodbye. Jennifer reached out and gave them both hugs and kissed them on their cheeks. Davie picked up Jenny and carried her out to the truck.

He made sure her seat belt was secure. He hugged Jimmy. Jimmy got in the truck and buckled his seatbelt.

He said, "Dad, I will help care for Jenny while we are gone."

After they pulled out of the driveway to return to Rosewood, Jennifer and Davie returned to the house. They sat on the porch in the lawn chairs, and neither spoke for a while.

Davie was hopeful Jennifer was finally starting to return to them. He knew he had to be careful and not expect too much too soon.

Jennifer was tired, but looking across the lake, the water was so peaceful and calm. Standing up, she said, "Davie, will you take me out in the lake in our canoe?"

Davie said, "Sure." Walking down to the lake, he watched her from the corner of his eyes. He knew she was experiencing a breakthrough today, but there were many more issues she would have to deal with in the days ahead.

When they reached the lake, Davie helped her into the canoe and pushed it off the bank, and he climbed in the canoe behind her. Taking the oars, he paddled out toward the center of the lake. The lake was so calm.

Jennifer said, "Davie, let us stop here in this lake spot. The sun had set in the distance, creating a beautiful glow across the lake. Moving a little closer to Jennifer, Davie was also enjoying the lake and how peaceful and quiet it was on the lake.

Suddenly, Jennifer rolled over the edge into the lake. Davie dove into the lake. He was unsure why she fell into the lake, but he looked for her in the water.

She came up beside him in the water. He reached out to her, and they returned to the canoe. He held the canoe steady and helped her back into the canoe. He climbed back into the canoe and wondered about what had just happened.

They were both wet, the sun was falling, and they needed to return to the bank. It would be dark soon.

He helped her back out of the canoe when they reached the bank. He got out of the canoe, pulled the canoe out of the water, and tied it to a post.

As they returned to the house, Jennifer saw a look of concern on Davie's face when she came out of the water.

After several months of pushing everyone away from her, she suddenly realized that he might be concerned about her fall into the lake and why she did that.

When they got back to the house, each got into the shower. When Davie got out of the shower, he made them some hot chocolate. When Jennifer joined him, he poured her a cup of hot chocolate. She took her cup and sat down on the couch. Davie filled his cup and joined her.

Jennifer said, "Davie, I am sorry if I worried you when I fell into the lake. The water looked inviting and soothing when we sat on the lake.

The water was cold but refreshing, and I felt clean for the first time. None of the showers after the rape made me feel clean. I felt dirty, filthy, humiliated, angry, and violated.

Today, I felt like I finally saw the light leading me out of the darkness. I heard you and mom talking about me. Your voice and the things you were saying helped me to wake up from this horrible nightmare. I felt like I had been gone a long time, and a lot had happened.

I looked at the pictures in our living room and realized I was not the only one who was hurt. Each one of you was also hurt by what the rapist did.

He took something from me he had no right to take. I resisted him in every way I could. The rapist forced himself on me. He beat me and would slap me if I cried out in pain. He hit me so hard that it almost caused me to black out from the pain. I must have blacked out the last time he struck me because everything went dark.

I had begged him not to do this to me. I told him I was pregnant and did not want to lose my baby. He got what he came for, but not because I wanted him to have it.

I entered the darkness when I regained consciousness at the hospital and learned I had lost my baby. I escaped from the physical and emotional pain I felt."

"Davie, how long has it been since this happened?"

Davie said, "Jennifer, it has been six months."

"Oh, my goodness, Davie, this means I have been in this dark forest of anger, disbelief, fear, humiliation, feeling degraded, dirty, soiled, and of no value to anyone as a wife, mother, or human being," Jennifer said.

Davie saw the tears flowing from her eyes. Hearing her describe what happened were only a few things she had to endure. He was glad she could finally speak of this.

Stay silent; you allow this man who raped you to destroy you and your chance for happiness, to feel he could treat any woman that way and get by.

The rapist took from her things he had no right to take. He not only got the sex he came for but also destroyed her in whatever way he could. He did not care that he hurt her because he would get what he wanted.

Now that Jennifer was finding the courage and strength to share some of this with him, Davie knew he needed to continue to listen and support her to help her through all of this.

It was up to her now to get whatever help she could and let God help her find a way to heal and recover. He was heartbroken knowing some of the things she had gone through from the rapist forcing himself on her.

He and the kids loved her and would do whatever it took to help her heal.

He knew the road to complete recovery would be painful for her. He could see the pain on her face as she tried to tell him the events of that horrible day.

Davie vowed to use whatever means to find this rapist and see him in prison. He had not only done all these horrible things to Jennifer, but the rapist had also attacked him, their children, and the family.

He watched Jennifer as she sat quietly, sipping hot chocolate. She had her head down and was crying.

Davie moved closer to her. He gently put his arms around her. She put her cup down and laid her head on his shoulder.

She cried and cried. Davie let her cry. The tears were streaming down his face as he held her.

She stopped crying and said, "Davie, how soon can you build us a bedroom at the back of the house?

I want us to have a bedroom for us. I do not want to return to that bedroom with all its horrible memories.

I hope you can turn our old bedroom into a nice guest room for mom and dad when they visit, friends or other families."

Davie said, "We will start getting the plans together right away. Your dad and my dad will help us. We will get it built much faster with our dads helping us. We need to get this done right away."

Jennifer said, "I think mom would enjoy helping me pick out paint and other things we need for our new bedroom. I am glad I can focus on getting this special room for us.

With the kids gone to mom and dad's, I want us to sleep in Jimmy's room tonight. I am tired of sleeping on the couch, and I know you are not getting much sleep on that cot.

Davie was ready for bed, and Jennifer followed him to Jimmy's room. She turned back the covers of the bed and slipped into a gown.

Sliding between the sheets, she saw Davie get in bed beside her.

Davie could feel the tension as he lay beside her. He reached for her hand, and she laid her hand in his hand.

Knowing this was a step forward, he told her, "Take your time because we have the rest of our lives together. This night tonight is a starting place for you in your recovery. I am so thankful to still have you with me, and I think tonight we should both get a good night's rest. I will see you in the morning."

He slipped his hand away, turned over, and went to sleep. Jennifer turned over and thanked God for being here for them. She drifted off to sleep beside the one she loved with all her heart.

The next morning, she could smell the aroma of coffee when she woke up and joined Davie for a cup of coffee.

CHAPTER 3

The Past and The Future

Looking out across the yard, Jennifer saw geese landing on the lake. It was fascinating to watch the geese. The birds were amazing. She loved how they moved so easily and graciously through the sky.

Feeling the effects of all she had been through recently, Jennifer felt extremely tired. She would be so glad when she felt energetic again and did not have such a heavy heart. She had two wonderful children she loved, and they needed her now and in the future.

She also had a loving and wonderful husband. She met Davie when she was fifteen and married when she was eighteen. They enjoyed a loving and wonderful marriage. Jennifer knew she owed it to Davie to do whatever she needed to, face the future, and put this all behind her.

Stretching out on the couch, she was asleep in no time. When she woke up later, she felt a little better.

Davie got a phone call from one of the officers he worked with at the police station. He went out on the porch to avoid disturbing Jennifer while she was resting.

When Jennifer awakened, she heard Davie talking on his phone.

He said, "Jim, I want to thank you and the other officers I work with for all you are doing and have done to help us get answers regarding this rape."

Jennifer decided to go to the kitchen and see if any of those good cookies were left. She was not hungry, but a cookie sounded good to her.

Jim told Davie he had been on the computer all day looking for leads or something to work with regarding Rick, the student Jennifer dated who tried to rape her.

He said, "I found the police report that Jennifer had filed with the police department regarding Rick's attempts to rape her. The police arrested Rick, and he had to appear before a Judge.

The Judge gave Rick a date to reappear in court for the trial. The Judge released him from bond after his mom paid the bail money needed to get him out of that horrible jail. She told the Judge she did not want her son to spend another day in that horrible jail.

Later he did not show up for the date the Judge had given Rick for appearing in court for the attempted rape charges.

A warrant was issued for Rick Goldman's arrest for failing to appear in court. That warrant is still active and on file. We tried to locate him to arrest him but never found him."

Davie said, "Jim, we will do first things first. We must find Rick, but we will continue searching for him and other clues.

We need a convincing case against him, both for his attempted rape of Jennifer and the suspected rape of her this time.

We know someone raped her, and we have good reasons to suspect it might have been him. We need to find the evidence needed to arrest him when we do find him.

Davie hung up the phone and sat quietly, thinking about everything Jim told him, and knew finding Rick would not be easy. Also, he needed facts to support arresting him for his attempted rape when he dated Jennifer and proof that he returned to get what he told her he would return and take advantage of her.

Jennifer cannot yet name him her rapist; they did not have much to work with. He knew he had to keep his personal feelings about all that had occurred recently to his wife and the loss of their baby so that he could use his skills as a detective with an open mind.

Inside, he heard Jennifer in the kitchen doing something. Going inside, he found Jennifer eating cookies and drinking milk, so he joined her.

Her mom certainly knew how to make good cookies. He was glad she was teaching Jenny how to make cookies.

Finishing his cookies, he returned to the living room, where they stored their old school albums and pictures of family and friends.

He found Jennifer's school album for the year Rick tried to rape her. It did not take long to locate Rick's picture in the album. Using his cell phone, he took a picture of Rick.

Jennifer entered the living room and saw Davie reviewing the old tool albums.

When she saw Davie take a picture of Rick, she went outside and sat on the porch. She knew Davie was a great detective and would find the rapist. She was still unable to talk about who took advantage of her. This would help Davie if he knew who did this to her. With his skills as a detective, he would find him. It was troubling to even think about what had happened.

Davie called his dad and told him that Jennifer wanted us to build a big bedroom and bathroom. She also wanted to take their old bedroom, where she had been viciously violated, and make it a guest bedroom.

Jerry thought building a bedroom for them would be great. He knew Jennifer could not face going into their bedroom after the trauma of what happened in that bedroom.

He told Davie, "Son, I would love to help in any way I can. I can call contractors here in town and find a contractor to start the project immediately. The contractor could do the things neither of us could because they need some of their tools and expertise."

Several days later, Davie called Jennifer's mom and dad and told them of his and Jennifer's plans regarding their house.

He spoke to Tom to see if he could still help do some things to help them get the job done more quickly.

Tom said, "You can count on us to help you. I am good with a hammer and basic tools and love building things.

Peggy would help with the kids and help Jennifer plan the rooms. She could help her pick out paint colors and furniture.

A guest bedroom would be great when we visit, are needed to help with the kids, or just to visit."

Jennifer called her mother later and discussed how her mom could help her.

Peggy was thrilled to see them build the new room on the house and was eager to help Jennifer with plans to turn their old bedroom into a nice guest bedroom.

After Peggy hung up the phone, she told Tom, "This building project is needed now. I believe it will be very therapeutic for Jennifer. I look forward to helping her with the plans and paint colors."

Peggy got their things together so they could return to Linkerville. She knew this could be particularly good for Jennifer, or it might be a setback for her depending on how things went during that time of building and purchasing things for the rooms. If problems created a setback for Jennifer, then Peggy would get samples at the stores and bring them back to show Jennifer.

Jennifer was eager for her mom to go with her. After she got there, she could help her pick out some things in town.

This was the first time she had left the house since leaving the hospital. She felt nervous and tense. Looking around as her mom drove to town, she felt uneasy and fearful.

She had never told anyone who had raped her. She feared that Rick, who raped her, might still be in town somewhere or nearby and come back and kill her. He had almost killed her with his brutal sexual abuse. He had taken her baby's life with his actions to get what he wanted.

Their first stop was a lumber company. She found the perfect flooring for the rooms. They found some other things for the bathroom Jennifer liked.

The prices were reasonable, so they got the price codes and information they needed to call the order in for selections.

As they were leaving the store, a tall man with blonde hair, wearing sunglasses, had gotten out of a red Corvette and was walking toward them.

Jennifer panicked, screamed, and ran back to their car. Peggy had to run to catch up with Jennifer.

They both got back in the car. Peggy reached over and locked the doors. She started the car in case they had to leave there in a hurry.

Peggy felt the man's appearance had triggered a bad reaction and fear for her daughter. She wondered if this man reminded Jennifer of the one who had taken advantage of her. The man reminded her of one who had dated Jennifer several years ago.

Jennifer was shaking and crying. Peggy did her best to calm her down. She called David and told him what had happened and what the man looked like.

Davie said, "I will be there soon. We will find the young man in the store and take him to the police station for questioning.

Several police cars showed up to assist Davie.

Peggy told Davie, "I am taking Jennifer back to the house."

Davie told her that would be best.

The officers who were on the scene were out of their patrol cars. Davie and an officer with him pulled into the parking area.

Walking into the store, they spotted the man Peggy had described. They read his rights to this young man and told him they were taking him down to the police station to ask him some questions.

The man was shocked when they told him this and knew of nothing he had done to break any laws. He told them he would go with them and cooperate with them but knew of nothing he had done wrong or broken any laws.

He pointed to his red Corvette car parked out front and asked that they bring him back here when they finished questioning him. When they arrived at the police station, he answered all their questions. He grinned and said, "I was here in town to celebrate our first anniversary on that date you asked about.

I kept the receipt to give to my wife so she could put it in the book she kept regarding our wedding.

He showed them the receipt, and the police were satisfied after they called the restaurant. When the police called to check the alibi, they learned he was a steady customer and had been there celebrating their anniversary on that date.

The manager said they loved coming there for the special breakfast they serve every morning. His records showed they had made reservations for a particular table on that date.

He said the young man and his wife are nice people; we often see them in our restaurant.

Davie was satisfied with the information and knew this young man was not the one they were looking for. Davie took him back to get his car.

He thanked him for his cooperation. Davie told him they were looking for a man who had violently raped a woman.

He said, "This woman was my wife, and we are trying to find this man."

Davie thanked the young man for answering the questions. He had a good alibi for where he was on the day of this assault.

The man got into his Corvette, turned to Davie, and said, "Good luck with the search for him. I cannot imagine how I might feel if someone did that to my wife."

Davie said, "I know how it feels because my wife was the one the man raped. She had a miscarriage because of his brutality."

The young man said, "I am so sorry to hear this about it being your wife and the loss of your baby. I am glad I cooperated with you. I wish I could have been of more help."

Leaving the parking lot, Davie called Peggy to check on Jennifer and let them know the young man they took to the station had a good alibi that checked out for what he was doing the day of the rape.

Peggy told him Jennifer had calmed down and was taking a nap.

Peggy called Tom on his phone and told him what had happened in town and how upset Jennifer became when she saw this man.

When Tom returned, he told her he would take the kids for ice cream. He did not think the kids needed to be in the house when they returned from town, especially with Jennifer upset. They usually got upset when the kids saw their mom upset.

Davie sat in his cruiser, not saying much. His partner Jim knew when Davie got this quiet, he usually thought deeply about one of their cases. Jim remained silent as he sat there in the police cruiser.

A few minutes later, Davie turned to the police officer sitting next to him, and he said, "Jim, Jennifer has been unable to tell us anything regarding the name of the one who raped her. We are unsure if she knew him or if he was a total stranger.

We know this man had a great alibi. The manager told us Larry and his wife were in his restaurant and had a good alibi for where he was the day this happened to Jennifer. He was very cooperative when we asked him questions.

For some reason, though, his appearance upset Jennifer. She became frightened and panicked when she saw this man. I cannot help but believe that his appearance is what frightened her.

This description is something I think we should consider while we are looking for the one who raped Jennifer. When we return to the station, we should follow up on a few things I have been thinking about.

We need to share this description with the other officers and let them know Larry, the one we took to the station, can be ruled out as a suspect. We need more information on Rick, who tried to rape her when she was a student in High School.

Jennifer told me about Rick after I returned home when my time of service ended with the Army.

Rick loved driving Corvettes and usually drove a new one."

Davie called Peggy on her phone and told her he would be working late on this case he was working on now.

He told her the one we took to the police station had a good alibi. He is not the one that we are looking for. We know his appearance was upsetting to Jennifer.

Tom and Peggy were grateful the police department had assigned Davie to oversee the rape case. He was a good detective. He would leave no stone unturned to find the rapist.

Hanging up the phone, Peggy's thoughts were about Rick and how much she and Tom were suspicious of him and his intentions when he dated Jennifer. He also drove a bright red Corvette like the one they had seen in town.

Peggy knew Jennifer was nervous about going to town. When this man came out of the lumber store, the sight of this man upset Jennifer. His appearance frightened her.

After they got home, Peggy decided it might be best to drive to town to pick up samples so Jennifer could choose the things she wanted and colors from them.

Jennifer had her first therapy session today. She knew she should keep her appointment after what happened in town today.

She asked her dad if he would take her to therapy while her mom spent time with her grandkids. Jennifer appreciated the family being here to help her with the kids and the house. The future was ahead of her, and she needed this therapy to help her heal and get on with her life.

He said, "Yes, I will be glad to take you to therapy and be there with you until your therapy is finished today.

You know how much I love you and want to see you be able to put some of this stuff behind you. What you are dealing with is something I know must be exceedingly difficult to cope with."

As Tom drove her to therapy, he thought about the stalker stalking her. The stalker had caught her alone and kidnapped her. No one knew where he had taken her. They had searched everywhere and could not find her.

Davie had finished his time in the service and came home. He had looked forward to seeing Jennifer. Tom remembered how Davie helped him, and with the skills he had learned in the Army, they found Jennifer.

He also remembered how frightened Jenifer was when the stalker kidnapped and held her hostage. Now she was dealing with the fear of the one who raped her coming back to take her life.

They arrived at the doctor's office, and Tom waited in the waiting room while she had therapy.

Tom decided to call Davie while he was waiting. He asked Davie if he was busy; if not, he wanted to talk to him for a few minutes. No one was in the waiting area, so he could talk freely.

Tom said, "Davie, I am here with Jennifer, and she is in therapy. I want you to know I am here to help you if you need my help finding the rapist.

I believe with all my heart it might be Rick who did this. I remember what he screamed out to Jennifer as they left the courthouse to take him back to jail.

Davie, I am glad you oversee the search for him. Peggy and I never liked that boy when Jennifer was dating him. Jennifer figured out for herself what kind of person he was and called him and met with him to let him know it was over between them.

We saw him for the person he was and were so afraid that Jennifer might not realize in time what kind of boy he was and he would hurt her.

He thought his nice car, taking her out to fancy places to eat, and buying her some jewelry gave him the right to get what he wanted from her.

He sure did not like someone telling him NO.

He had told her he would be back and get what he wanted from her. Peggy and I see what it is doing to Jennifer, and all of you are going through.

If you see something I can assist you with in searching for Rick, please let me help you. I feel so helpless not being able to do much to help all of you. I know our being there and helping with the kids, meals, and house is a lot of help, but I want us to find Rick, get the answers, and prove he did this to Jenifer.

While we are working on the house, I wanted to see what you thought about me taking Jennifer and the kids to my mom and dad's and letting them stay with them. We would all be there together, and you could join us after you got off from work. None of us need to be breathing the dust from the drywall. I know mom and dad would love having all of us. Peggy will help mom in the kitchen."

Davie said, "Tom, that is an excellent plan. Let me know if your mom and dad are up to our stay there for a few weeks. Jennifer and the kids would love being there for a few weeks. That was always Jennifer's favorite place to go. She loves her grandparents."

Tom said, "I will call them and let you know if we will stay with them."

Jennifer had about fifteen more minutes with the therapist, so Tom called his mom and dad.

Charlie answered the phone. He was thrilled to hear Tom's voice. Tom asked him if they would stay with them for a couple of weeks while they worked on Davie and Jennifer's house.

Charlie said, "Yes, we are up to having all of you and looking forward to your visit with us. We are both doing good for old folks. It would be great to spend time with all of you. We know Jennifer and Davie have been going through a lot lately. We know about what happened to our granddaughter and the loss of the baby.

When are you planning to be here?"

Tom said, "After all Jennifer went through, they decided to build another bedroom on the house for them. She has been unable to go into their bedroom after she got home from the hospital.

Building a new bedroom would help her. They plan to turn their former bedroom into a nice guest room. The contractors will start working next week.

We will take the kids home this weekend, get some more clothes, and return and take Jennifer and the kids to your place Monday morning.

Charlie told him that was great and glad they could help some by everyone being there with them. He looked forward to everyone coming. He could hardly wait to tell Bea the good news.

Jennifer returned to the room with a more peaceful look, so the first therapy session must have been helpful.

When they returned to Jenifer's house, her mom and Jenny were fixing supper. Jenny loved doing things with her grandma in the kitchen.

Tom told everyone after Davie got home about the plans for them all to go and stay with his mom and dad. Jennifer was thrilled with the plans. She loved being with her grandparents, and the kids enjoyed their time there.

Saturday morning, Tom told the kids to get their things together so they could spend the weekend with them in Rosewood. The kids were thrilled and started packing their things.

Peggy ensured Jenny and Jimmy got what they needed for a few days. The kids were ready to go.

Davie told them he would take Jennifer for a nice long drive. When he said that, Jennifer was unsure about leaving the house for a long drive. She remembered something the therapist had told her: "Davie, that will be nice."

Monday morning, Tom and Peggy drove back to Linkerville with the kids. They enjoyed having them with them over the weekend.

They would pick up Jennifer, get more clothes for the kids, and head to his mom and dad's place. Davie would join them that evening after he got off from work.

Jimmy was sitting in the back of the truck singing, "Over the river and through the woods to great-grandpa and great-grandma's house we go."

Charlie was sitting on the porch watching. They were both so excited about the visit. Hopefully, being there would be good for their granddaughter Jennifer, whom they loved so much.

It was special having their son, wife Peggy, their granddaughter and Davie, and those precious great-grandkids for a visit. She had made some cookies for them.

Jennifer was concerned about how safe it would be at her grandparents' house. She was still worried the rapist might return. She told Davie about her fears, but he reassured her that they would protect her and the kids with their lives.

Charlie walked down the steps and onto the sideway when they arrived. He had hollered at Irene to tell her everyone was there.

Jennifer loved their home place, bringing back good memories of her and Davie getting married in this house. Looking up at the curved stairway, Jennifer remembered coming down the stairway in her wedding gown and tripping on the edge of her gown. She had tumbled down the remaining steps into the arms of her dad, who was waiting for her.

She would have taken a nasty fall if he had not been there. Thankfully, she was only a few steps from the end of the staircase. When she fell, she popped a few buttons off her wedding gown.

The wedding music stopped when she fell. They delayed the wedding to give her grandma time to sew the buttons back on her gown; lots of good memories are here with her grandparents.

The kids found which bedroom would be theirs while they were there. Tom and Jimmy would share a room. Peggy and Jenny would have another bedroom. Davie and Jennifer would have one of the bedrooms upstairs.

Jimmy Joe loved spending time with his grandpa. His great-grandpa was a lot of fun, and he loved the farm.

Jenny spent time in the kitchen with her grandmother and great-grandmother.

Davie was spending late hours trying to track down some leads for the rape case. He joined them in the evenings after he got off from work. He was so glad that they were all at Charlie and Irene's.

He used to be their neighbor. That was how he met Jennifer. He had gone down to check on Charlie and Irene after heavy snow to make sure they were okay, and milk the cow for them and gather their eggs so Charlie would not have to get out in the bad snowstorm.

When he had pulled into the drive, he saw Jennifer out in the snow, and she looked like an angel in her white snowmobile suit. She came over to say hello, and he told her he lived next door and had come to milk Charlie's cow and gather the eggs.

When they went inside later, Irene insisted he stay and eat supper with them. He could not take his eyes off Jennifer. Everyone would think he was crazy for falling in love with her at first sight.

After Davie got off work, he drove over to check on how things were coming along with the renovations and additions to the house. He was amazed at how much they had done.

Walking back down the hall, he stopped at what used to be their bedroom and opened the door. He was pleased with the transformation of that room.

Davie drove over to Charlie's, and when he arrived, Jenny came running up to him and said, "Look, Daddy, great grandma taught me how to sew a button on a shirt."

Davie scooped her up in his arms, kissed her, and told her she had done an excellent job.

Looking up, Davie saw Jennifer standing there. She was smiling. Once again, the memories of her, the first time he ever saw her, came to his mind. Despite some sadness in her eyes, he could see her love for him, which melted his heart.

Sitting Jenny down beside him, he reached out his arms to Jennifer. He held her gently and kissed her on the cheek. He suddenly remembered kissing her on the cheek before he left the first time he saw her.

Jennifer saw that cute look on his face after he kissed her on the cheek and said, "I remember the first time you ever kissed me on my cheek. We had just met that evening here at Grandpa's house. Davie smiled and took her by the hand.

They joined the others inside the house. Jimmy ran to his father and told him about the adventurous things he had done with his grandpa and his great-grandpa Charlie.

Peggy saw a little bit of glow on Jennifer's cheek. It was the first glimmer of something other than pain, and it made her feel things would be better; it would take time for healing.

Another week, he brought more dramatic changes in both rooms. Uncle Joe would have been thrilled to see the changes. He had done an excellent job of trying to keep things updated and useful.

Now, he and Jennifer were adding their touch to make it even more useful, especially right now. The things that Jennifer had picked out from the samples looked great. The paint colors were soft and soothing and nice colors for bedrooms.

Davie noticed how much room they had in the new bedroom for them. He knew Jennifer would be pleased. He was eager to show her their bedroom when it was finished.

Moving home day had arrived. The family packed up their things. Davie and Tom put them in the vehicles. It had been a wonderful place to be with family. Everyone got their hugs. The kids and Jennifer thanked Charlie and Irene for their wonderful visit.

The kids rode with their grandma and grandpa back to the house. Davie and Jennifer were alone and had some time together before returning home.

Jennifer told Davie that she was so excited about the new bedroom. She told him she was nervous about seeing their old bedroom again. She dreaded opening the door to that room.

They had the contractors paint and add shelves to the kids' bedrooms. The kids would love their new bookshelves.

Tom, Jerry, and Davie had worked on the house's addition. They wanted to help get some things done before the contractors started. They wanted to finish the work right but as quickly as possible. The contractors did the work they needed to do on the addition.

Jerry had been there daily, checking everything and ensuring the contractors followed the plans.

Davie and Jennifer were pulling into their driveway at home. He knew she would be pleased with all the changes made in the house.

The kids ran to their rooms and came out of them, saying, "Dad, Mom, we love our new shelves." They returned to their rooms, and Peggy smiled as she watched them put their things on their shelves.

Tom told Davie to stick close to Jennifer and that he would unload the suitcases. They were all concerned about her and what her reaction would be when she opened the door to the guest room.

Davie took Jennifer's hand and walked down the hallway to their new bedroom.

When he opened the door to their room, she had tears in her eyes and a smile on her face, and she loved their new master bedroom. It was even nicer and prettier than she could imagine.

The room was so big, and the furniture they picked out was perfect for that room.

Walking into the bathroom, she saw a large shower for Davie, a big soaking tub for her, and two sinks in the vanity. It was perfect in every way. The room felt comfortable and peaceful.

They left their bedroom and started back down the hallway. Jennifer stopped and did not know if she could go another step. She knew she had to find the courage to open that door to their old bedroom where she had been raped.

So much pain was in her thoughts of the events of her being raped in that room. She had talked to her therapist about that room. Her therapist had given her some things to think about so it would help her when the time came to take that next step in healing.

Davie did not rush her. He gave her some time to think about things. He knew she could see it again if she could not go through those doors this time. Kissing Jennifer, he whispered, "If this is not the time to go to the room, we will wait. If you want to do it today, we do it together, whether today or another day."

Jennifer remembered the counselor's words and a scripture Grandma Irene had told her in (Psalms 37: 39-40) she had shared with her during their visit. "The salvation of the righteous is of the Lord; he shall deliver them from the wicked and save them because they trust in him."

Jennifer knew her grandmother was right. Her grandmother trusted God and reached out in faith that he was there as promised, and she would be okay in his care and the love of her family.

Turning to Davie, she said, "We will do this together. I love you and want to move on from everything in that room. If it is too much, when we go into the room, I will leave the room."

Holding hands, Davie opened the door, and they walked slowly into the room.

Jennifer had prayed before she entered the room and asked God to help her overcome the anger, pain, and suffering Rick had caused her and the loss of her child so that she could move on with life.

She would never forget the precious baby she lost. She would always remember her baby, and it would take time to heal from that horrible event, but with God's help, she knew she could have a life again with joy and happiness. This was a step towards healing.

Jennifer closed her eyes when Davie opened the door. Opening her eyes, she was shocked. The room was beautiful, and the colors she and her mom had chosen were perfect.

The old room was gone and replaced with this beautiful guest bedroom.

Walking toward the bed, she motioned for Davie to sit by her. They sat on the edge of the bed while she took in the transformation of this room.

She bowed her head for a moment and thanked God for being with her during those moments when she had been filled with fear and pain. She knew it was time to move on with life.

Davie took her by her hand, and they walked into the bathroom. There was a big shower stall her dad would love.

The double sinks and a nice commode sat up slightly higher. It was the perfect guest room. As they came out of the bathroom, she noticed the loveseat, table, and lamp,

A nice chest for their folded clothes was on one wall, and the closet had double racks to hang clothes on. She told her mom and dad to see this room.

She said, "This is your room now, so you will have your room when you visit. I love mom and the things we picked out for this room. It is beautiful!

She hugged her mom and her dad. Then she hugged Davie, cried, and said, "Thanks, everyone, for giving me back a room I no longer dread or hate. It was a room filled with many painful memories, but now it is beautiful."

Jennifer knew this room was a starting place in her life and a chance to move on with her life.

She knew it would take much more than this room for complete healing, but what a beautiful beginning.

She would continue to go to therapy for a while. This therapist had helped her before and was helping her now.

Jimmy and Jenny got out cookies and milk for everyone. Great grandma Irene had told them to bring those cookies home and share them with everyone today. It was nice standing around in the kitchen, munching on cookies.

Peggy got the kids ready for bed. They would be sleeping by themselves in their bedrooms tonight. Peggy had enjoyed spending time with her granddaughter. Jenny had been so sweet about sharing her bed with her grandmother while staying with her and her brother. Now that she and Tom had the guest room, they would enjoy being in the same room together.

Jimmy was already in bed when Peggy checked on him. He was growing up so fast. He was an incredibly nice boy. He had a nice personality and reminded her a lot of his dad.

Davie was an only child but was raised by good parents, who taught him many things that helped him become the wonderful person he is today. He was sure good to Jennifer and his two kids.

Kissing Jimmy on the cheek, she told him good night.

After completing her tasks in the kitchen, Jennifer made her way to Jenny's bedroom. There, she lovingly arranged items and kissed her goodnight. As she surveyed the room, Jennifer couldn't help but admire the perfectly installed shelves that suited Jenny's needs perfectly. The shelves showcased an array of cherished dolls and other belongings that belonged to Jenny.

Jenny gave her mom a sweet kiss and gentle hug and said, "I love you mom, and I am so glad you are going to be okay.

I missed you while you were in the hospital, and Grandma and I prayed for you daily."

Leaving Jenny's room, she checked on Jimmy. She thought he was asleep, but he grinned and said, "Fooled you, mom, you thought I was asleep."

Jennifer smiled and said, "Yes, son, I thought you were asleep, but I am glad you are not. I can tell you how much I love and appreciate you lovingly caring for your sister and helping your grandma and grandpa during this time."

Kissing him on the cheek, she walked out of the room, and a tear trickled down her cheek as she thought of how blessed she was to have two wonderful children.

Tom was already in their new guest bedroom. He was already in their new bed when Peggy came to bed. She crawled in beside him, and Tom hugged her and told her how proud he was of her and glad they could help Davie and Jennifer.

Davie loved his new shower. It felt so good standing there with water running over him. He was proud of the new master bedroom. Finishing his shower, he dried off and found Jennifer getting ready for bed.

It was great having their bedroom again. The room looked so nice. The colors she and her mom selected were soft and gave the room a warm feeling.

It was the perfect master bedroom, and it looked great. Turning back their covers on the bed, she slipped into their bed.

When Davie got in bed, Jennifer scooted over closer to him.

Davie reached for her hand and held her hand ever so gently. Neither one spoke as they lay next to each other.

The light in the bathroom cast a soft light in the bedroom. Davie looked at Jennifer. Her eyes were filled with love for him but very tense.

He loved her so much and knew he would need to continue to be patient with her.

Jennifer lay next to Davie, wishing all that had happened to her would vanish from her mind.

Once again, she wanted to enjoy physically their expressions of love for each other. Right at that moment, she felt such love for him. Still, her body was filled with so much pain and discomfort, and the rape haunted her mind to be able to express her feelings physically.

Davie gently pulled his hand from hers and said, "Jennifer, I know how much you love me. You know how much I love you. I am just thankful you survived all you have been through and are still here with me.

I almost lost you, and we did lose our baby, but we still have each other and our two wonderful children. Together, we will move on to the future.

Right now, it would be best if you had time for healing. Recovery takes time, but you are seeking help from your therapist and can let us help you with our love and support. You are also turning to God for help.

We have the rest of our lives to devote to each other and express our love physically. Still, right now, we both need our rest, and you need to be able to reach out to me without all this pain and suffering. I am here for you always.

What we have for each other is special; together, we will face what tomorrow brings. You are not alone, and I will be here beside you."

Jennifer reached up to his face and touched the face of someone she loved very much. She wanted to come to him, healed and ready to be his wife. She appreciated his love and understanding. She kissed him on his cheek and said, "I love you, Davie."

Davie said, "We need to get rest tonight and see if we like this new mattress we will be sleeping on. The old mattress was getting soft, but this one is firm but comfortable.

"I love you too. Good night, my sweet, dear, precious wife." Davie rolled over and was asleep in no time.

Jennifer said her prayers and began to feel sleepy. Waking up the next morning, she said, "Thank you, God, for bringing Davie into my life when I was just fifteen.

He is a wonderful person, husband, and father to our children."

Crawling out of bed, she showered and dressed for the day. She found Davie in the kitchen. He had made coffee and poured her a cup. He kissed her sweetly and said, "Good morning, sleepy head."

Davie noticed Jennifer seemed more relaxed, and he knew the good night of rest had been good for both.

They took their coffee and donuts from the cabinet and walked to the porch. Everyone else was still asleep, so they sat on the porch and enjoyed the morning breeze. Some fish were flopping in the lake. Neither one spoke.

They sat and enjoyed their coffee and donuts.

Davie had been watching Jennifer out of the corner of his eye. Jennifer was getting tense.

He did not know that Jennifer had been sitting on this porch when Rick drove up in the driveway. Davie had been careful not to talk about the rape or push her to tell them what happened and if she knew who had done this to her.

He said, "I called the office and told them I would arrive late today. I am eager to do more research on this case I am working on now. As you know, the captain assigned several officers to assist and help me."

Before Davie could say any more, Jennifer turned to him and said, "Maybe I can help you also if you are working on my case to find the one who raped me."

Davie moved his lawn chair so he was facing her more and sat back in the chair. He was unsure if Jennifer was ready to start talking about this. If she was ready, he was glad he was there for her.

Jennifer also turned her chair to face Davie. She said, "Davie if anyone can find my rapist, it is you.

I know it must be hard for you to locate the one who did this to me. He also took our baby away from us. Please find him, arrest him, and put him in jail.

He does not need to run free to molest someone else."

She paused for a moment and took a sip of her coffee. Reaching for his hand, she extended her hand and held on tight to Davie.

She said, "Davie, the man you are looking for is someone I know. He is the one that tried to rape me when I was still in High School.

I told you about him when you got out of the Army.

When he was arrested and had to appear in court, he said he would return to get what he wanted from me.

The morning he raped me, he was there to get what he promised he would get from me. He took something from me; he had no right to take it from me.

You and our family need time, love, and support to help me heal. I refuse to let him continue to destroy what we have together and hurt our children and you. I have been hurting all of you with my anger and frustration from the pain of losing our child.

I need to continue in therapy and appreciate your last night's love and understanding of my condition.

Thank you for supporting me and for always being there for me. I am so glad I have you in my life. I can also count on God to be there for me.

Grandma Irene has shared some things I feel are truly helping me. She has shown me some scriptures I can also turn to and how important prayer is in my life now and throughout life."

Davie leaned back in his chair. He was thrilled she could finally find the strength and courage to tell them who raped her.

Davie stood up, and Jennifer also got out of her chair.

Davie said, "Sweetheart, I am glad you could find the courage and strength to share this with me. I know talking about this is not easy right now.

Knowing who did this to you is the help I needed to continue with some research I have been doing.

Now we know for sure whom we are looking for. I promise I will find him, bring him back to face what he has done to you, and let the courts decide his punishment.

Doing my job as a detective will be foremost in my mind as I work on the case. I know I must keep my personal feelings in check to find, arrest, and bring him back."

Davie reached over to hug her. She wrapped her arms around his neck and cried. It was a relief to have been able to tell Davie. He continued to hold her in his arms and let her cry.

The sound of two kids in the house reminded them that two kids would be looking for them.

They opened the storm door for Jennifer and joined the ones in the kitchen. Peggy was making pancakes for everyone. They decided that sounded good, and Jennifer offered to help her mom make the pancakes.

Jimmy had been watching his mom. He said, "Mom, are you okay?"

Jennifer washed her hands and dried them. She leaned over to her son and said, "Son, how could I not be okay with everyone in this room loving and helping me get better." She gave him a big hug and bent over and hugged Jenny.

Jenny was eating her pancakes soaked in syrup. She stopped eating and gave her mom a very syrupy, sweet kiss on her cheek. Jennifer loved getting love from her children.

She brought the big stack of pancakes to the family, and they all enjoyed the pancakes and some bacon and sausage Peggy had cooked.

As he looked around at his family, Tom took everything in. He knew that his daughter must have had a little breakthrough. He saw a glow on her face and a twinkle in her eyes.

Somehow, his precious daughter was finding within herself what it would take to move on with life. He dropped his head down and silently thanked God for this precious family.

Davie finished eating, stood up, and said, "I need to go to work. I have a lot of work to do regarding this case I am working on, and I hope all of you have a good day.

He kissed Jennifer and whispered, "Call me if you need to talk to me today. Thanks for being my precious wife."

Tom walked with Davie outside.

Tom said, "Davie, thanks for loving and caring for our Jennifer like you have since you first met her.

No one could have had a better man married to our daughter. So glad you have each other.

We will be here a while longer, and thanks for fixing up that great guest bedroom. We slept well last night. It is sure a nice room. Love the shower we have in our bathroom."

Davie said, "Before I leave, I want you to know that Jennifer found within herself the strength to share with me who raped her.

Our suspicions were right. It was Rick. I must get busy, find him, and bring him back here. I promised Jennifer I would let the courts give him his punishment, and I would remain the detective. I cannot let personal feelings interfere with my work. I will have to work long hours, so I'm glad you can be here a little longer for Jenifer and the kids.

I do not know how we would have made it without you, Peggy, and my family. Bless you, Tom, for being such a wonderful dad for Jennifer and a great father-in-law for me."

Davie left for work, and Tom returned to the house. He had some plans for the kids.

Tom called Jerry and asked if he would like to join him and the kids for a day away from home.

Jerry said, "That sounds great. I will come over there.

Marilyn thought she would come with me and see everyone today. If that will not interfere with Peggy and Jennifer's plans."

Peggy told Tom, "Tell Marilyn to come over; Jennifer and I would love to see her."

Marilyn had not been to the house since the room was added on. She loved the new bedroom. She was so proud they built that room in the house.

Peggy showed her the guest room and said it is for all of us to use, and if you and Jerry want to come over and spend the night here, you will have the guest room you can use.

When Peggy showed her the guest room, she could not believe what a nice transformation the room was.

Jennifer wanted to take their sandwiches down to the lake. They fixed a basket with the things they needed for a real picnic.

They spread their tablecloth on the ground and sat and enjoyed their lunch. It was so peaceful.

Jennifer turned to Marilyn and said, "Thank you for letting the kids come and stay with you that weekend that I was raped. I was so thankful my children were not home.

I appreciate what you, Jerry, and my mom and dad have done to help us deal with this. We always knew our kids were being well cared for by their grandparents. Thanks for your prayers and for being there for us.

This morning, I was talking to Davie before he left for work. I knew he was trying to locate the man who raped me.

I found it within myself this morning to tell him who did those horrible things to me." She stopped for a moment to wipe a tear from her face.

"Mom and Marilyn, the man who almost took my life and took the life of my unborn baby is Rick."

Marilyn and Peggy had been in that courtroom when Rick stood before the Judge for attempted rape. They remembered his warnings and what he said.

They were relieved to know for sure who did this to Jennifer. The pain brought to each of them when she was raped was hard to deal with.

Each one stood up, and they all hugged each other. They all were in tears, but knowing who did this to Jennifer was a relief.

Gathering up their picnic basket, they headed back to the house. Jennifer said she was tired and thought she would take a nap. They both saw relief in her face and pain from all that had happened.

After Jennifer laid down in her bedroom for a nap, Marilyn and Peggy sat on the porch and talked.

They also took a few minutes to hold hands and pray. They knew God was with them and their families. He had been there for Jennifer. Marilyn was so thankful she and Jerry had gotten the kids for that weekend.

Jerry and Tom were having so much fun with the grandkids. Jimmy and Jenny were good kids. Of course, after the little adventures they had gone on, they had to stop and get ice cream.

CHAPTER 4

Hard to Locate the Rapist

Davie left that morning and headed to work, knowing who raped his precious wife. He knew finding Rick would not be easy, but he had a good group collaborating with him.

He had some things he wanted James to feed into the computer. He hoped they produced some clues. James was good on the computer. It helped that someone else like James could help him with the research needed on the computer.

Chief Roberts heard Davie enter the station and called to join him in his office. He wanted to talk to Davie. He called out to Davie to come to his office as he needed to ask him some things. Davie sat down inside the office.

Chief Roberts said, "Davie, I know this has been a tough time for you with everything that happened to Jennifer. If you need time off from work, let me know. I will give you time off when you need that time at home.

We appreciate your work here at the station and as an investigator."

Davie said, "Jennifer had a moment of a breakthrough today when she finally talked to me about who raped her.

She told me she knew I was assigned to oversee that case. Jennifer said she was glad I had been chosen. She knew I would approach it as an investigator who never let personal feelings interfere with his work.

My suspicions were right when she told me Rick, who had tried to rape her when she dated him in High School, showed up at the house that day and forcibly, against her will, raped her.

She told me she tried to get away from him. She resisted him every way she could, but he was too strong for her. He slapped her with such force and brutality that it caused her to black out and later miscarry the baby.

Jennifer told me to find, arrest, and bring him back to let the judges determine his punishment. She had been afraid to name him as the rapist, for fear he might still be around close somewhere and kill her.

Now that we know who committed the rape, I will start working with the knowledge of who we are searching for."

Davie found Officer James in their office doing some research on the computer. Davie shared with him that Rick was the one they suspected. Now, we can start the search for him.

Officer James said, "Great and so proud Jennifer could find the strength and courage to help us by naming the rapist.

When Davie got home from work, Peggy hugged him and said she knew who the rapist was because Jennifer had also shared the name with her and Marilyn.

She said, "I know you are a good detective, and you will find him no matter what rock he is hiding under, regardless of how far you must go to get him and bring him back.

While talking to you, I thought of something that happened when Jennifer and I went to town.

She saw this man with sunglasses and blonde hair, and he had gotten out of a red Corvette. Rick always drove Corvettes. Since it upset Jennifer so much, I wondered if Rick looked like that when he came here that morning. The neighbor said the car she saw was red."

Davie said, "Thanks, Peggy, for reminding me of the event because I can use some tools we have at the office to take a picture of Rick, turn his hair blonde, and put sunglasses on him. I know exactly what the man looked like because I spent time checking out his alibi. I will check on that in the morning."

Not seeing Jennifer, he started down the hall to their bedroom. She was sound asleep and never knew when he got home. Seeing her sleeping so peacefully, with Jimmy on one side of her and Jenny on the other side of her, was special. Jennifer had her arms around them. Easing the door shut, he returned to the living room.

Jimmy woke up first. He eased off the bed and was careful not to wake his mama or Jenny.

He was so glad his mom was doing better. He and Jenny wanted to be sure, show her lots of love, and help her while she was feeling bad. Jimmy knew his mom was sad because of the loss of her baby. Jimmy and Jenny had looked forward to having a baby sister.

He did not like that mean man being so mean to his mama. If he had been here, the man would not have been able to hurt his mom. He would have called the police if he had been here. The police would have come and arrested that man.

He knew his dad would find that mean man, and he would have to spend time in prison for what he did to his mama and baby sister, who died.

He heard his dad talking and was glad he was home. He also enjoyed spending a lot of time with his grandma and grandpa.

Davie turned around, and there was Jimmy. Grabbing his son up in his arms, he hugged him. He looked down, and Jenny had her little arms reaching out to him, so He picked her up, too.

Jennifer had awakened and came down to the kitchen. It was a beautiful picture of Davie with a kid in each arm.

Walking up to Davie, she said, "I believe you have your arms full, so I will come back later for my hug." She kissed him on his cheek and kissed both of their precious children.

Jennifer knew her mom and dad planned to return to Rosewood after they ate. She told them she would take care of the dishes when they finished eating. Leaving earlier would help them get home much quicker and miss a lot of the heavy traffic. Her parents planned to return in the morning.

Jennifer appreciated them being here to help in many ways. She had wonderful parents.

Davie helped her put away the food, and Jimmy put the dishes in the dishwasher. The kitchen was clean in a brief time.

Davie found a good show to watch on tv. Jimmy joined his dad because he liked that show, too.

Jenny wanted to show her mother some things in her room. Jennifer joined her daughter in her bedroom.

Jenny brought her mom a piece of paper. She had drawn some pictures on it and printed her name and the words, "Mom, I love you."

The picture she drew was a good sketch of a mom, dad, brother, grandparents, and great-grandparents. Under the pictures were "Best grands and great grands."

She had drawn a stick man and a sketch of a little girl sitting on his knee. She wrote, "Love you, daddy, and mom."

Jennifer picked her precious little Jenny in her arms and, holding her close, said, "I am so glad you are my little girl. I love you too."

Tom and Peggy woke up early the next morning at Davie and Jennifer's house.

Jennifer was still in bed because fatigue came easily from all she had been through.

When Davie arrived at work, he had Officer James feeding things into the computer to see if they might get some leads.

Davie thought getting a search warrant for Rick and his parent's house in Rosewood was a good place to start.

Davie stopped by Chief Roberts's office and told him that; Jennifer had told him who raped her. It was Rick, the one that tried to rape her once before. He told the chief about what had happened in Rosewood regarding Rick's attempted rape of Jenifer.

He said, "I must take a few days off here and go to Rosewood. I hope I might get some leads there to help me search for Rick and what country he may have fled to."

Chief Roberts told him to take whatever time he needed.

Davie left and arrived home after being approved to take some time off from work.

He told them he was going to Rosewood and see if he could turn up something they could use in their efforts to find him and bring him back to the USA to stand trial here.

Tom and Peggy assured him they would be here for Jennifer and the kids while he was gone and let him know if something changed here he needed to know about.

Packing a few things, he spent time with Jennifer before leaving for Rosewood. She assured him she would be okay and thanked him again for trying to find Rick and bring him back to Linkersville.

Arriving in Rosewood, Davie took his things to Tom and Peggy's house and would stay there for a few days. He left there and drove to the police station.

Everyone was thrilled when he walked into the office. They all stood around her talking to Davie when Chief Taylor entered the room.

Chief Taylor was happy to see Davie standing in the middle of the commotion in the front office. He approached Davie and said, "It is great seeing you here. We have missed you.

So sorry to hear about the loss of the baby and the horrible things that happened to Jennifer.

When they made their way to his office, Chief Taylor said, "What brings you to Rosewood? Does it have something to do with Jennifer being raped?"

Davie said, "Yes, I know you remember well the case of Rick, being arrested for the attempted rape of Jennifer. A few days ago, Jennifer finally talked about the rape. She told me she wanted me to know who raped her so that I could find and arrest him.

I am here hoping to find clues as to where Rick is now. I know everyone tried to find him when he did not appear in court for a hearing to be scheduled for his attempted rape charges, but he was a no-show at court.

If you have some spare room for me, I might need to use one of your computers. I know you have some state of art computers I used when I worked here."

Chief Taylor said, "We have an office you can use, and it is set up well with a computer that will be helpful."

When Chief Taylor took him down the hall, he said, "You can use this room."

Davie grinned when he saw it was his old office when he worked here. Walking into the room, he sat down at one of the computers. He spent many hours feeding material into the computer in search of answers.

He said, "This is perfect. Thanks for the office space."

Chief said, "I will have someone in records pull the files on Rick and bring them to you. If you need anything, just let me know, and if we can help in any way, we will gladly help."

Davie sat at the desk, and someone quickly arrived with Rick's files. He took some time to review the files.

The first thing he wanted to do was bring up a picture of Rick. He wanted to change his hair to a blond-haired person. Then, he wanted to create a picture of him with blonde hair and sunglasses.

The picture he created looked just like the young man that had frightened Jennifer the day she and her mom had gone to town. No wonder it frightened her so badly. A good disguise of Rick.

Picking up the phone, he called for records in the hospital, where they took Jennifer the night Rick tried to rape her. He could get some information from the evidence they collected when they examined Jennifer that night.

He drove over to the hospital and picked up those records. Then he decided to locate the address on the files where Rick lived.

He rang the doorbell at the Goldman house since a car was sitting in the driveway.

The lady who came to the door told him she was the housekeeper. She was nervous and wanted to know who he was.

He had shown her his badge, but she wanted to call and make sure he was who he said he was. She called the police station, and they assured her he was a real police officer.

Davie asked her if she had heard from the Goldman family and if they still owned this house.

She said, "Yes, this is their house, and they pay me to come and clean the place. They own quite a bit of property besides this place.

They want me to clean it in case they want to come here for a while."

Davie said, "Have you seen or heard from them recently?"

She said, "No, they send my check for cleaning to a bank here in Rosewood. I have not heard from them since they left."

Davie said, "If something needs to be fixed here, do you have a way even to contact them so you will know what they want to be done here?"

She shook her head no. She told him they had left in a hurry. They still hang many clothes in the closets, so they will return soon."

The housekeeper told Davie she only came to clean this house twice a month.

She asked him if he would mind checking out one of the rooms she had vacuumed. She told them it looked different than when I cleaned that room. It was their son's room."

Davie said, "Since you have some concerns about changes in one of the rooms, I will call and ask for one of the officers here in Rosewood to join us. Together, we can check out your concerns."

Reaching for his cell phone, Davie called Chief Taylor. He told him he was at the Goldman's house. He wanted to know if the Chief and a few officers could join them.

He said, "The housekeeper is here and has concerns about some changes in one of the rooms since the last time she cleaned the house."

Chief Taylor said, "One of our officers will be there in about ten minutes."

When the officer arrived, he showed the housekeeper his badge, and she let him in the house. Davie and the officers followed her upstairs to the room she was concerned about. They stepped inside the room.

You could tell someone had been there. The bed was hastily made. The bathroom had been used, and toothpaste was in the sink.

The housekeeper said this bathroom was spotless and now look at it. It did not look like this the last time I cleaned this room.

Davie said, "I think we will thoroughly check out the bedroom while we are here.

He opened a drawer in the dresser. To his shock, he found buried in the drawer some photos. He took a couple of pictures with his cell phone of the photos in the drawer before removing them.

Officer James was there with him. Picking up other photos, they found Rick with some other young girls. They took pictures of each one of the photos with their phone camera."

Davie called Chief Taylor and asked him if he could come and join them at Goldman's house.

While they waited for Chief Taylor to join them, Davie told the housekeeper she did the right thing by letting them check out the house.

Chief Taylor brought a search warrant with him so they could do a more thorough job of checking out the whole house. When Davie showed him the photos, the Chief was glad Davie called him.

Davie turned to the housekeeper and said, "Did you know Rick had been in court the day the family packed stuff and left here?

She said, no, I did not know they were planning to go anywhere until Rachel called me and said they would be gone for a while.

She wanted me to keep the place clean while they were gone. She did not want to return to a dusty, musty, smelling house.

They have been gone for some time now. They continue to deposit my checks into an account with my name on the account at our local bank.

Davie continued checking Rick's bedroom and found photo albums in the closet. There were also a few empty hangers on the rod in the closet. Things had been hastily moved into the closet.

Chief Taylor and Davie had Officer James check for fingerprints on some photos. Davie turned a page and found a photo of a half-dressed young girl lying on the bed.

He turned away from the photo and shook his head. The Chief said, "I will check these albums for you. I am finding more pictures of young girls."

This was a sick man who took these pictures of these young girls.

He was thankful he had found no pictures of Jennifer after Rick knocked her unconscious.

They had a search warrant and an active warrant for Rick's arrest. They took the photo albums. as evidence for the courts.

Officer James, Davie, and Chief Taylor wondered if Rick had left Linkersville and returned here that day.

The housekeeper was curious about why they wanted to take the albums and were interested in Rick. The Chief of police told her that Rick had done some things that were not good and against the law, so he had been arrested.

The day he appeared in court, his mother paid his bond money so he would not have to return to jail while waiting for the next court date the judge gave him.

He was supposed to return to court again for his schedule. Rick never showed up for that second court date. We have an active warrant for his arrest.

His mother called you to tell you they were leaving and for you to take care of the house after Rick had paid the necessary bond money.

The Housekeeper said, "Oh my goodness, I did not know those things had happened. His mom is rich and spoiled her only son. I understand now why they left in such a hurry. If Rick did not return that day, I feel someone has been here in this house."

The rest of the house checked out okay. They decided to check the garage.

The three of them and the housekeeper made their way to the garage; Chief Taylor opened the door to the garage.

Everything looked okay, but Davie noticed the lid was not on the top of the garbage can. He walked over to straighten the lid.

He raised the lid and noticed something in the garbage can. Wearing rubber gloves, he pulled a garbage bag out of the can.

The housekeeper told them all those cans had been empty, and garbage pick-up stopped after they left. With rubber gloves, they opened the bag. Inside were some jeans and a shirt. You could see some stains on the clothes.

The housekeeper said, "That is Rick's shirt and pants."

They returned the clothes to the bag and tagged the bag's evidence for court.

Chief Taylor thanked the housekeeper for letting them search the house and alerting them to the possibility that someone had been in the house since the owners had left.

She told them her name was Helen. She thanked them for checking everything for her. They asked her if she would like to have an officer circle the area and keep an eye on things.

She said, "Yes, that would be nice. Can I call you when I am here working so you can come and make sure the house checks out?

They told her to let them know when she would be there working, and they would send an officer there to check out the house for her.

She thanked them and said she needed this job to help pay for her husband's medical bills. He was in a bad accident, and it left him bedridden. It was spooky, though, walking into a house no one lived in.

When Davie, Chief Taylor, and Officer James arrived at the police station, they went to their offices, and each one started feeding information into the computers.

Chief Taylor got on his phone and started checking out some other things. They had brought back some good evidence. They were glad that Chief Taylor joined them, Glad he could get a search warrant so quickly.

Chief Taylor hated having files that were no longer needed but had never been closed. He used to give those files to Davie when he worked there. He was the best Detective they ever had.

Seeing him sitting in his old office looking for leads to find Rick, who had raped his wife, was good. He knew Davie would not let his personal feelings get in the way of doing his job. Plenty of proof was needed to establish Rick as the rapist in court.

The photos they brought back would help establish Rick dating several girls, and photos of those girls and some made of him with these girls would be good evidence of Rick's behavior regarding sex.

Looking into the families of these girls would take time, but it is worth talking to these girls if their parents consented.

Davie called Peggy on her phone. He asked about everyone, and she said they were all okay.

He also asked her if they could stay with Jennifer and the kids one more night. She told him they could stay for as long as he needed them to be there.

Davie thanked her for giving him their garage door code so he could let himself into their house.

He also told her he might need to stay more than one more night but would call her about his plans.

Peggy asked if he was having any luck with finding leads. He told her they had one good lead they wanted to check out right away.

Peggy said, "We pray you find the proof you need for this rape case. Thanks for calling."

Davie said, "Tell Jennifer I love her."

Peggy said, "She was tired. She decided to lie down on her bed and went right to sleep. I will tell her when she wakes up."

The next morning, Davie drove over to the police station. He walked into Chief Taylor's office. He wanted to talk to him about what they had removed from Goldman's house.

He was glad the Chief had brought a search warrant they could use to search the house.

They had obtained the right to gather evidence from the house for a trial when Rick was located and returned to the USA for trial.

The next thing they needed was the records of e next thing they needed was the records of when Goldman's private jet had been used for flights during the period surrounding the date of the rape.

Chief Taylor said, "Davie, I will take care of that for you."

Davie wanted to go to Rosewood Library. They kept a copy of each year of the school albums.

He planned to take copies of the photos of the girls Rick had dated or was in the photo. Davie wanted to match them up with school photos.

Ms. Grigsby saw him when he entered the library. She had heard about Jennifer losing her baby and asked about the twins.

She told Davie to let her know if he needed help finding whatever he was searching for.

After several hours of looking through the albums, Davie found photos matching some of the photos he had brought.

Returning to the police station, Chief Taylor motioned him to join him in his office.

He told Davie, "We might have a lead that will be helpful. We could see the flight log books of Goodman's private plane. We noticed the plane was fueled and ready for takeoff the night before the court date. The pilot did not log their destination when the plane was ready for departure.

After departure, the plane did not return to Rosewood until

Later. The plane logs showed only one passenger for this recent flight. There are no records of any flights scheduled since that recent flight.

I suspect if the one person flown here was Rick, he did not take the private plane to return to wherever he lived in some country. I also suspect Rick might have used a fictitious name and flown a commercial flight.

I know you will check out these things as you do your investigative work."

Davie said, "I appreciate the events you found in those flight logs and will indeed check out the possibility a commercial flight was used after the time he raped Jennifer.

I spent some time in the library today and found matches with some of the students in the Rosewood school albums in some of the photos. The graphic photos are very disturbing.

I shudder to think what my precious wife was going through when Rick raped her. The bruises and other things showed he was brutal to these girls, and he knew he had been brutal with Jennifer. And he figured Rick had also been very brutal with the young girls in the photos based on what he saw in the pictures.

He wanted evidence of how Rick treated these girls and his wife. This evidence helps to support that Rick needs to serve time in prison for the rapes and abuse Jennifer and these girls suffered from Rick."

Chief asked Davie to show him the photos again. He was sad as he pointed out the ones he knew as local students in Rosewood High School. Several girls were young and still in Jr. High at that time.

Some other photos were of girls who went to school in some of the surrounding towns. There were names on the back of these photos, so locating them by their names would be possible."

Chief Taylor sat back in his chair, dropped his head, and silently prayed for these young ladies.

Looking up, he told Davie, "We need to find Rick and stop him from hurting anyone else. There were photos of Rick with these girls who were half dressed."

Davie shared with the chief, Taylor, his plans for moving forward with this information.

After Davie and those assisting him in this search found addresses for some of the girls, they contacted the parents and asked if they could come and speak with them. Some met the officers, denying their daughter could have ever done what he had shared with them.

After their denials, Davie showed them the photos of some girls and their daughters. He explained to them that they knew

Rick was capable of raping someone, and they were fearful that their daughter might have been one of his victims.

Davie said, "We know he can be brutal when he rapes someone. We are not certain yet if the girls in these photos were drug-induced, without their knowledge, before being raped.

Some may have given their consent for sex to Rick. We know one person, Rick raped, who not only did not give her consent but resisted him with everything she had. He raped her anyway.

We only want to talk to them with you present and permitting us to see if they could share with us what happened in this photo of them with Rick.

Davie left the phone number of the police station with them and told them that if they learned some things that might be helpful to us, we would appreciate a call.

More evidence of Rick's behavior toward these young ladies helps us get him arrested, and he will have to appear in court.

At the next house, where Rick stopped, the parents were genuinely concerned about what Davie shared about Rick.

They told him their daughter had dated a rich boy there in school, Rick. They could not recall his last name.

They said, "This person you told us about sounds like the one that dated our daughter. He had a red Corvette, and his name was Rick.

We were not impressed with his car or the fact he was known as the richest boy in school. We were concerned about how well he treated our daughter.

We were relieved when our daughter told us she had no plans to date him anymore. When we asked her why she broke up with him so soon after dating him, she did not want to discuss it anymore.

Davie said, "I hate showing you these pictures we have of him, but when you see the picture of your daughter and Rick, you are right to be concerned.

I know what he is capable of because he recently raped my wife. The rape caused her to lose our unborn baby.

I am only here, though, as a detective to find enough evidence to support our concerns about how many young girls might have been raped by him even though they resisted with everything they had to try and stop him from raping them.

I am not here for any other reasons other than making sure he is caught and punished by the laws of our land for committing these acts and stopping him from hurting any more innocent women or young girls.

Rick also tried to rape my wife when she was in High School. Had a man not seen what was happening and stopped Rick, he would have succeeded at that time.

Raping her recently was Rick's revenge on her to let her know no woman or girl ever says "NO" to him."

When Davie showed them the picture of their daughter with Rick, they said, "Yes, this is the one our daughter dated."

Our daughter has received love and support from us. We had encouraged her to report this to the police when she told us Rick had raped her. She told us she was afraid to report him for fear of what he might do to her later. She asked us not to report it either because they feared he might return to hurt her again. We have kept quiet.

Therapy helped our daughter, after the rape, to be able to get on with her life. She is doing okay now, but we fear what it might do to her if she voluntarily spoke of this to the authorities."

Davie said, "I respect your daughter and the two of you. Her name will not be among those whom we have listed. Glad she is doing better and wishes her the best in life."

They said, "Yes, and we hope you keep your promise to keep our daughter out of this investigation. We would only consent if she were here and wanted to help."

Davie left his card with them, so they had his phone number if their daughter ever wanted to talk to him about being raped by Rick.

Davie left their place and marked that one as not available for any more considerations of help.

Chief Taylor said, "I appreciate how you managed these matters when you spoke to the families you talked to. We will consider that girl's struggles to get her life back together. We will not pursue her any in the future for information.

I will repeat that Rick must be found. He is a menace and dangerous person. He needs to be stopped before the next victim is killed.

He almost killed Jennifer and succeeded in being so brutal that it took the life of your unborn baby. We must find him, no matter what it takes."

Davie returned to his temporary office. Before returning to the computer, he wanted to talk to Jennifer. He called her phone, and she answered.

He told her he was having some success finding leads but would need to be here a little longer to follow up on these leads. He told her he missed her and would return home with her as soon as possible.

Jennifer told him, "Davie, I am making it okay. Mom and dad are helping me, and the kids love having them here. We will be okay, and I miss you too.

My therapy session was a good one today. It was helpful to hear some of the things she suggested to me.

I will do whatever it takes to put this all behind me so you and I can have a future filled with happiness and the love of our children. I have a lot to be thankful for. You do whatever it takes to get the information needed.

Please be careful, and I will not ask questions about your work. You are good at what you do, and we will be here when you return. I told Chief Taylor, "Hi, and thanks for his help."

Davie fed some information into the computer after he got off the phone. He needed to check out some local business places, restaurants, and business places where Rick might have been.

Davie knew from the work done that jewelry, flowers, and places to eat were often places Rick went with a date or bought flowers for his date. He liked impressing them by taking them to expensive restaurants.

He became aware of Rick's actions after he came back home when we had been in the Army. Jennifer had told him about Rick when they started dating again.

Feeling tired and sleepy, Davie shut down his computer and headed to Tom and Peggy's home to get some rest.

Morning came, and Davie picked up the phone and called his house. Jennifer was still asleep, so he asked Peggy if the kids were up yet. She told him they were awake and eating cereal. He asked her to put them on the phone, and she took the phone to them.

Jimmy said, "Dad, I am glad you called us. We love you. Thanks for what you are doing to help Mama. Mom is doing better, and Jenny and I are helping Grandma and Grandpa while you are gone."

Davie said, "I love you too. I appreciate you and Jenny being such good kids and helping care for your mom, grandma, and grandpa.

Being a detective searching for the truth, I can count on you when I am away. Hand the phone to Jenny now so I can tell her I love her too."

Jenny got on the phone and said, "Daddy, I love the shelves in my bedroom. Thanks for those shelves. You can come to my room when you get home and see everything on the shelf. I love you, Daddy. Bye."

Peggy got the phone, and Davie said, "Thanks for being the wonderful parents you are and grandparents. I appreciate you being there for them so much while I am in Rosewood. Thanks also for letting me stay at your house.

I wanted to let you know I am finding some clues that may prove helpful in finding a place to start locating Rick.

It is not easy to do this job with my personal feelings because of what Rick did to Jennifer. What happened to Jennifer somehow helps now on how to approach some of the people he has also raped. I feel their pain, knowing what it has been like watching Jennifer trying to deal with her pain and emotions regarding being raped by Rick and losing her baby.

Thanks for all your help. Will be in touch again later. God bless you both!

CHAPTER 5

Help Needed

Getting much-needed rest, Davie was ready to head to the police station. He was eager to work on the computer.

Chief Taylor nodded at Davie when he arrived that morning. He was checking with a couple who often flew to Europe. This couple was wealthy.

They knew all the best places to go over in Europe. They know where you go and when you want to be left alone and in a private place.

They also had their private jet, which they used when they traveled to Europe. They called the station when they were going on trips and asked for a patrol car to check on their place while they were gone.

When Chief Taylor told them why he was calling them and the kind of case his officers were working on, they were eager to help him with whatever information he needed regarding Europe.

They told him the best restaurants, car rental places, and places to visit while you were on vacation. They even told him the names of the places where they rented a place so they could stay for a while.

She also mentioned one town they enjoyed visiting when they traveled to Europe. They always enjoyed the peace. It was a very private place. The security is great. You can feel safe when you are there. Not a lot of people know about this small town exist. Of course, when you want to be out in public again, there are towns nearby where you can shop and eat in nicer restaurants.

The airport is not exceptionally large and is mostly used by people like them, who have jet planes.

She said, "I hope some of this information is helpful. I hope you find whomever you are looking for, Chief Taylor."

Davie contacted the FBI regarding his wife's rape case. They seemed glad he called them and would be looking into the matter, and they would get back to him later.

Later in the day, to everyone's surprise, FBI agents walked into the police station, showed their IDs, and asked to speak to Davie Vaughn and Chief Taylor.

The clerk up front- paged Chief Taylor and Davie Vaughn to come to the main desk.

They left their offices and met in the hallway. Neither one knew why they were paged.

Davie was glad the FBI was there. They might be able to help them with some things they had learned in the past few days.

Chief Taylor invited them to join them in his office.

The FBI shared some current information they had obtained regarding the case Davie had previously shared with them; they were extremely interested in hearing more about the case.

The FBI said, "After I hung up from talking with you, Mr. Vaughn, I fed that information into our computers and investigated the facts concerning this case. We produced a few leads that might be helpful in this case.

We are offering our help to assist in locating this rapist. We are glad you spoke to us about this rape case. We are eager to help you find Rick Goldman and put him behind bars.

Chief Taylor mentioned what he had learned from a couple who also traveled to Europe.

FBI agent said, "Some of the information we found regarding a Rick Goldman and this town mentioned by that couple fit in with some of the information we have and, certainly worth checking out.

We have a Jet at the airport, ready for the flight to Europe. We would like Davie Vaughn to go with us if he is available and can go on this European trip. I know he would like to help us find the one who raped his wife, and we offer our condolences, Davie, for losing your baby girl."

Chief Taylor said, "Davie Vaughn is free to travel with you. Thank you for offering him this opportunity and your offer of help regarding Rick."

Davie said, "I appreciate your help, and thank you for allowing me this chance to help in the search for Rick.

I will call and let my wife and family know I will travel to Europe. They are all eager to see Rick arrested and put behind bars."

Davie called home to let them know he would be flying to Europe to check out some leads regarding Rick.

Jennifer said, "Be careful. I will be praying for your safety."

Davie drove to Tom's home to pick up a few things he would need for the trip. The FBI agents followed him to the house and headed to the airport.

Once they were in flight, Davie showed him the photos they found in their search, which they had managed to get from Goldman's house with a search warrant.

The agent listened to the information they had gathered so far about Rick.

The agent said, "Davie when we arrive at our destination in Europe, we will be met by some undercover agents whom I have had contact with regarding this case. We have been working on some of the leads we shared with us.

I understand why finding Rick is so important to you, Davie. You are the husband of one of the rape victims. I need you to let me be totally in charge when we arrive.

This man needs to be found and stopped. He has molested young girls, some of whom were not of age.

We have followed your work, Davie, and it was done very professionally. You were on the right track in searching for Rick.

We want you with us when we locate and arrest Rick, but we need you to let us oversee the arrest.

I know you will continue collaborating with us as a detective here to arrest someone who needs to be behind bars and not let your personal feelings interfere with whatever needs to be done.

We have the authority here in this country to arrest and take him back to America for trial."

The plane landed. A black car was waiting for them at the airport.

Davie felt blessed and fortunate to have, in our country, an agency like the FBI. These agents put their lives on the line daily yet are so committed to their work.

Their first stop was a very prominent restaurant. The server took us to a table that had been reserved for them.

The agents were relaxed, and you would think they were all here on vacation and having the time of their lives. They were joking around with each other and even the server. Nothing in the restaurant went unnoticed. Yet no one in the restaurant seemed to know or suspect they were being watched.

Davie joined in the conversation. They had given him a disguise in case they saw Rick. They did not want Rick to see Davie and try to flee the country.

Leaving the restaurant, they drove to a residential neighborhood, which was probably where the rich and famous lived.

The homes were huge and magnificent. Some places were nice places where people could stay while on vacation.

Davie was asked to remain in the car with Agent Harry while the other two agents rented one of the Condos.

While waiting in the car, Davie spotted a new Red Corvette nearby. He did not get a good look at the driver from their distance.

Davie told the agent about the car that looked like the kind of car Rick drove.

Agent Harry called the agents inside the building and casually talked to them. The agents returned quickly to their car. They pulled away casually and drove down the road. They spotted the red Corvette up ahead.

Agent Harry placed a call to alert some other agents in the area that they had spotted a red Corvette up ahead with license plates that matched what they were looking for.

Davie noticed the Corvette pulled in front of a nightclub. An incredibly young and attractive woman got in the car. The Corvette drove off.

A couple of other cars with the agents whom they had been called joined them in no time.

They surrounded the Corvette, and with a loudspeaker, the driver was told to pull over and put both hands on the steering wheel.

The agents left their cars, and with guns drawn on the driver, they instructed him to exit the car with his hands in the air slowly.

With their research, they knew this was the one they were looking for, and he was using the name Jeffery. They had traced his name to the Corvette they had just pulled over.

Agent Harry remained in the car with Davie. He knew from their information regarding Rick Goldman that this was the car and the one they had been looking for.

Davie watched all the action from within their car. The car had tinted glasses, so no one could see him, but he could see what they were doing.

The agent showed the red Corvette driver his credentials, read Rick Goldman his rights, and handcuffed him.

The young woman in the car was shocked when they stopped them. She had only dated him a few times.

The agents told her she needed to call someone to get her. They got her name, address, and phone number. They wanted this information if they needed to talk to her again.

Rick screamed at her and told her to call his mom at this number, he shouted to her. He was furious when they handcuffed him.

He refused to tell the agents anything. He wanted his lawyer. He knew he was dealing with the FBI and was in trouble.

As they drove back to the airport, Davie had seen Rick up close enough from inside their car to know they had arrested the right one. He might be calling himself Jeffery, but it was Rick. Davie felt sad and even angry because this man had damaged his wife for life and was responsible for losing their unborn baby girl.

The agent who was sitting in the back seat with Davie said, "We deliberately left you in the car because we each knew that if this man had done that to our wife and caused the loss of our child, it would be hard to come face to face, and not feel some rage inside.

You showed us your willingness to allow us to take care of this arrest, and we were glad you got to see this arrest made and know he will not be hurting any other innocent victims.

You are a very resolute detective who does not let personal feelings interfere with your work. We were pleased we could apprehend him without creating a big scene.

Davie said, "Yes, I felt rage, but most of all, I felt the peace of mind, knowing the one who raped my wife would no longer hurt anyone else or be able to hurt her again.

I appreciate your taking the case and letting me come with you to find and arrest him. I could see him through the windows of this car, and you got the right man."

When they left Europe on their plane, Rick did not recognize Davie. Davie was still in disguise. He sat quietly in the back part of the plane.

Rick was handcuffed to the arm of the seat where he was sitting. He swore at them and was furious he was being taken back to the United States.

After the plane landed, another car was waiting there for them.

Chief Taylor and another officer were in one of the Rosewood Police cruisers. One of the agents rode in the police car with Rick handcuffed to him. Another police car was at the airport in case they needed more assistance. The agents had complete control of the situation.

Davie rode with the other two agents in a rental car they picked up at the airport. When they arrived at the Rosewood Police Station, other officers were there, ready to assist. They put Rick in one of the more secure settings in the jail, away from the other prisoners. They wanted to be able to watch him closely.

Once Rick was locked in the jail, the agents wrote up their reports and thanked Chief Taylor for letting them take his detective with them.

They had nothing but praise for Davie, his research, and his professional approach to this exceedingly challenging task.

They also commented on the excellent work The Rosewood Police Department is doing.

Turning to Davie, the agent said, "Davie, if you ever want to work with the FBI, let me know. We would love to have you with us. You are an excellent investigator and detective.

We already had agents stationed in Europe, where we learned Rick might be. We could arrest him as soon as we arrived because the other agents had been there earlier to check out some things for us.

I am glad it went off smoothly, and I appreciate you letting us do the job we are qualified to do regarding the arrest of Rick.

You would have managed everything okay, but we knew we could spare you from dealing with Rick one-on-one when we arrested him.

Thanks for contacting us and allowing us to help you find and bring him back here to Rosewood.

The agents shook hands with Chief Taylor and Davie and left.

Davie said, "Watching them in action in Europe was special. I am glad I was there with them. Before we arrived, The work they did helped make this job possible in less than 24 hours."

Some families whose daughters had been raped by Rick came to the police station the following day.

Chief Taylor invited them to his office, where they could talk privately. He asked Davie to join them.

Once they were seated, Davie told them about his trip to Europe thanks to the help of the FBI.

Davie said, "We are happy to tell you Rick was found in Europe. They arrested him and brought him back to the USA.

He is in jail here under tight security until he appears before the judge. Since he fled the country, it is doubtful the judge will release him on bail now."

The mother of one of the daughters said, "We came here today to let you know our daughters will appear in court to testify against Rick. When we told them about your visit, they wanted to help you by being witnesses.

They were sorry to hear Jennifer, a girl they knew when they were in High School, had been raped by Rick. They remembered when she was in school, they heard some boy had tried to rape her, but some man had stopped him before he could rape her. They also remembered what a nice girl she was.

Our daughters remember, too, what they went through when he raped them. They wanted to help by being witnesses, too."

The mother's stood up, and each hugged Davie and told him how sorry they were about his wife and losing their unborn baby.

Davie was in tears and glad they were willing to help, but they also realized what this would be like for those girls and their families when they appeared in court to testify.

When the ladies left, Davie and Chief Taylor returned to his office. They were glad they had the help of the FBI and could bring closure to the attempts to find Rick and bring him back here to Rosewood.

Davie called Jennifer. He said, "I will be home tonight. I have much to share about my trip to Europe with the FBI.

I am leaving the station and will pick up my things at your mom and dad's house and head home. Love you, and see you soon."

When Davie got home, Jimmy and Jenny had already gone to bed. Jennifer greeted him with a hug and kiss.

Her mom and dad had waited up for him, too. They also hugged him, and everyone was eager to hear about the trip to Europe and what had happened.

Peggy fixed them something to drink, and they all sat around the dining table with Davie, sharing events leading up to going to Europe. He told them about the FBI and his contact with them.

He said, "The FBI showed up at our office and said they had been looking into this case after I had contacted them.

They knew they could help, so they came to Rosewood.

They shared some things they had learned about Rick when they fed information into their computers.

We told them about information Chief Taylor had learned about a place in Europe. When we shared this with the FBI, they said it matched some of the things they had found in their research.

He told us a jet was waiting at the airport for them and asked Chief Taylor if it was okay to make me with them.

He said the FBI would be the ones in charge while in Europe. He told me they had the authorization and all the paperwork needed to arrest someone in that country and bring them back to our country.

When we arrived, we ate at this nice Restaurant. They had brought a disguise for me so there would be no danger of Rick recognizing me. I learned later Rick liked to eat at this place. The FBI agents there had done much investigative work before we arrived.

They knew what kind of car he drove and what name he was using. He used the name, Jeffery.

When we arrived there, I thought we might be there for several days or weeks. The agent in charge had found us a Condo that we could stay in while we were there.

Within less than 24 hours of arrival in Europe, they had arrested Rick and brought him back in their jet plane that was fueled up and ready for takeoff."

Jennifer said, "What did Rick say to you when he saw you?

Davie laughed and said, "The disguise for me was good, and Rick never knew who I was. I was in the same plane Rick was in, but he never figured me out.

I sat in the back of the plane and never spoke a word.

Rick is back in Rosewood jail, a special confinement jail away from the other prisoners. It is very doubtful the Judge will allow him to be released from jail on bond this time after Rick fled the country when he was under bond.

While I was in Rosewood, I got to use my old office to work at the police station. Seeing all the officers who worked there when I was there was great."

Jennifer got out of her chair and hugged Davie. She said, "Davie, you found the stalker, and now you found Rick, and I am glad you located him."

She hugged him and thanked him.

Davie said, "I got a lot of help from Chief Taylor and the other officers and am grateful for the help from the FBI. I was surprised when I contacted the FBI with our case that they would help us and come to the precinct.

They even offered me a job with the FBI and said they were impressed with my detective skills and how professional I was.

The FBI had taken the information I sent them, and with the tools they work with and the workforce, they found Rick much sooner than I could have.

They could also go over there, arrest him, and bring him back here. We got Rick back in jail before he got wind of us looking for him and fled to another country.

One other part of this detective work that Chief Taylor helped me with was going to Rick's home in Rosewood. He got us the needed search warrants and joined Officer James and me at the house.

When we arrived at the house, the housekeeper was there cleaning the house. We showed her our badges, and she let us in the house.

Before we could even tell her why we were there, she told us she was glad we came because she thought someone had been in that house since the last time she cleaned it. She was paid to clean it every two weeks.

She wanted us to search the house well. We called Chief Taylor and told him the housekeeper had invited him inside the house. She thought someone had been in the house since she cleaned it.

Chief Taylor had told me to wait for him, and he would get a search warrant to search the whole place. Officer James was with me. The housekeeper was a nice lady and was glad we were there.

Chief Taylor arrived. She told him she wanted him to search because she knew him. He told her they remembered her and would like to check the house for her.

She told them the bedroom upstairs was where she wanted to be searched first.

When we got upstairs, she told us it was Rick's room. Things did not look messed up, but they began the search.

Chief Taylor and I looked in the closet. We found empty hangers, and stuff had been tossed in the closet.

Jennifer, I saw some photo albums. We all had gloves on, so Chief Taylor got the albums down. We started looking through the albums, and I walked away.

There were pictures of Rick with several different girls. Several other pictures caught our attention, so we took those as evidence. We left the bedroom and checked the rest of the house, and everything was okay.

I told the Chief I thought we ought to check the garage. When we walked out into the garage, I saw a trash can with the lid not sitting on the can particularly well.

I walked over to the can, and as I lifted it, I saw a bag inside it. The housekeeper said she did not know why that was in the can.

The house owner had her stop all garbage pickup after they left. I set the cans out for them to empty and then called and stopped them from picking up the garbage.

Chief Taylor and Davie pulled the bag out of the garbage can. Inside the bag were some jeans and a shirt.

The housekeeper said those things were some of Rick's clothes. We put them with the other evidence we collected. The things I shared with you tonight will help make a case against Rick.

The photos we found will also help the case against Rick, but I will not describe that because it is something on which we are still working.

Davie said I am tired, and I am sure you are too. Glad we were able to get some evidence and got the rapist in jail.

I am ready to crawl into our bed with my sweet, beautiful wife and get some rest."

Tom and Peggy went to the guest room. They were so proud of Davie and the work done to help find Rick.

CHAPTER 6

Rapist Found

Jennifer was thankful that Davie and the FBI were able to find Rick and arrest him. His being in jail after he had been brought back from Europe gave her some peace of mind. She had been so afraid he might come back and hurt or kill her.

Jennifer was proud of Davie, the other officers, and the FBI, who helped find Rick.

She had been praying for Davie when he told her he was flying to Europe to assist in locating and arresting Rick.

Knowing all the things Rick had done to hurt her and her loved ones, she knew this must have been difficult for him.

The realization of having to appear in court to testify against Rick and what he did to her when he raped her would be difficult. The therapist had spoken with her about this in her recent therapy session.

Reading her bible more had brought her closer to God, and she was eager to return to church. She wanted her children to grow up in church and be taught God's word. She and Davie had both grown up in church.

When the stalker held her hostage during the last semester of her senior year, she relied on prayer and scriptures to help her while in captivity.

Her family and friends prayed for her, just as Davie's family had been praying for him when he was in Special Forces in the Army.

He had been captured and held in captivity for a lengthy period. The Army sent him help once they could determine where he was in captivity.

They rescued him, and he could return to his unit in the Army. When his enlisted time was up, Davie came home.

Jennifer recalled what it was like when Davie got home. When he learned the love of his life, whom he hoped to marry, was missing and held against her will, he was ready to look for her.

Davie, using many of the skills he had learned in Special Forces, made it possible for him to locate and rescue me.

This time, Davie had been searching for someone who also needed to be found and punished for the horrible things he had done to me, with his brutal raping causing me to have a miscarriage. Davie was patient with me during this grim time of recovery from being raped and losing our unborn baby.

She loved Davie so much, and he was not only a wonderful husband but also a wonderful father to their children.

When she talked to Davie about the church he grew up in and told him she wanted them to get started going to church again, he was thrilled to know they would be going to his home church.

Davie called his mom to ask if they still had Sunday School at 10 a.m. and church at 11 a.m.

She told him "Yes" and was thrilled to know they would be going to their church.

Davie still had a lot of his friends going to that church. Jennifer had learned that some of her friends would feel right at home with a wonderful pastor in that church.

CHAPTER 7

Court Date Set

Chief Taylor called Davie, and he said, "Rick's mom and dad are back here in Rosewood. The housekeeper called to let me know they were home.

Rick's mom called today and said she would visit her son. I told her she could see him, but one of us would be present.

Since she had sneaked him out of the country before, she was someone they felt could not be trusted to abide by the laws.

Rachel was unhappy about those arrangements but still wanted to see her son and talk to him. His lawyer would be with her. The visit went without any problems.

When she spoke to Rick, the lawyer had to remind Rick's mom about what she could and could not do according to the law.

A court date has been set for Rick to appear before the Judge.

I will keep you informed as to what is going on here. Thanks for helping us finally catch Rick and get him behind bars.

We miss you, but you are doing an outstanding job in Linkersville. Oh yes, something else happened this week that I almost forgot to tell you. We learned later from the Judge's office that Rick's mother had seen the Judge and tried to get him out on bail. She said she would pay whatever it took to get her son out of jail.

Judge Baker called and told me about Rick's mom approaching him with offers of enormous amounts of money if he would let Rick out on bail.

The Judge said, "I laughed and reminded her that her son had violated the law when she took him out of the country.

I also told her I had read the case that would be coming up in a few weeks, and based on all I had read, I would not grant him a chance to be bailed out of jail, no matter how much she offered or tried to bribe him.

The judge also told her she should have brought her attorney, and he would have told her the penalties for trying to bribe a Judge.

The Judge said He called us to let us know she would try almost anything to get Rick out of jail.

He wanted us to tighten security with extra patrols until Rick appeared for his court date.

He also told us not to allow any visitors to visit him without several officers present. He was to be kept in his cell, and visitors would see him there under tight security, with only his attorney being allowed to enter his cell until his court date.

When Davie got home from work, he shared with Jennifer what Chief Robert had told him.

He said, "Jennifer, Rick will not get out of jail with his mom paying bail money. He will face charges for leaving the country and what he did to you and those other girls.

Some of these girls will appear in court like you will be testifying against Rick and telling their stories. His punishment will include the rapes of these young girls, some of whom were underage.

I hope this will help ease your mind concerning Rick. I am so proud of you for your progress in therapy. I will be glad when we can put all of this behind us and move on with life."

Jennifer woke up the next morning feeling the best she had felt in quite some time. She was physically feeling stronger and ready to start a new day. She was also relieved that Rick's mom could not get her son out of jail by paying an enormous amount of bond money.

Jenny and Jimmy came running to her and said, "Mom, can we go outside and fly our kite's dad got us?

She said, "Yes," and I want to watch you outside."

The kids hugged her and went outside.

Jimmy got his kite up quickly, but Jenny was having trouble. Jennifer remembered the days of flying kites, so she helped Jenny get her kite up in the air.

The kids were having an exciting time. They would run and watch their kites flying in the air.

They stopped when the wind died down. The kites were not flying well.

Jennifer said, "I think we should get some ice cream."

Jimmy said, "Mom, do you feel like getting out and driving the car?"

Jennifer hugged him and said, "Son, I will be okay and want some ice cream. You and Jenny will be with me. My doctor said I was doing great. It is time to leave the house and enjoy doing things with the family."

Jennifer got her keys. She texted Davie and sent him a message letting him know she and the kids were leaving to get ice cream.

He texted her back, saying, "Can I meet you there and have ice cream too? Jennifer showed the kids her text from their dad.

The kids said, "Text Dad! We would love to have him come to our favorite place to eat ice cream."

The ice cream was great. Davie also told the kids we would all attend church this coming Sunday, where Grandma Marilyn and Grandpa Jerry go to church.

Jimmy said, "That is a great church, Dad. Jenny and I go to church with them when we visit them."

Sunday, they all loaded into the car and headed to church. The kids saw their friends, whom they had met before when they visited the church.

Davie and Jennifer were met with hugs and made to feel very welcome. The church had been aware of what this family had been going through and praying for them.

The message the pastor preached was so uplifting and inspiring. Jennifer felt God's presence in ways she had not experienced.

She thought of her grandparents and how much they relied on God as she sat there listening to the message from God. She looked forward to returning the next Sunday.

When they got home from church, they received hugs from the kids, and the kids thanked them for taking them to church today.

The remarks from their kids humbled them, and both vowed that they would keep going faithfully to church every Sunday.

Davie knew he would have to miss some when his work took him out of town, but Jennifer could take them to church.

Peggy and Tom came up for a visit. They were missing their grandkids and Jennifer and Davie.

They were thrilled to see the changes in Jennifer and how well she was doing.

The grandkids ran up to them and hugged them. They also told them they would be going to church every Sunday now.

Tom and Peggy were thrilled to hear this. They knew Jennifer and Davie had gone to church off and on. Tom was glad they would be going faithfully to church.

The church would be able to offer their support to them, in special ways, when Rick's trial started. This would be a rough time for this family.

When Tom and Peggy asked if they could spend the night, the grandkids said, "Yes."

Jennifer said, Mom, Dad, I love it when you visit. Thanks so much for all your help during this rough time in our lives.

I am so glad we fixed our old bedroom into a guest bedroom.

Now you have a special room to call your own when visiting."

When Tom and Peggy returned to Rosewood, they talked about selling their house to Bobby if he still wanted to buy it. They loved their time with these grandkids.

Peggy and Tom had visited with his parents before they came home. Charlie and Irene were getting older and having health issues.

They wanted to be closer to them so they could offer their help if needed.

Tom's brother did not live near them, and even though he loved his parents, he spent little time staying connected with them.

Tom knew he was the only one his parents could count on for help.

Later that day, Peggy called Bobby. She said, "Son, I am calling to invite you here for supper. We also want to talk to you about something your dad and I have been discussing. Will tell you more tonight if you are free to come over and visit tonight."

Bobby said, "I will see if Evelyn has any plans for tonight and call you back."

He called back and said they would gladly join them for supper.

Peggy fixed a great meal they all enjoyed. After the food was put away and the dishwasher loaded, they gathered in the living room to visit.

Tom said, "Bobby and Evelyn, you mentioned once that you would love to buy our house if and when we decided to sell it. We want to sell this to you if you still are interested, and we are buying ourselves a home in Linkersville.

Our time with our families has shown us that being closer to them in Linkersville would be great.

We would find a home there close enough to offer my dad and mom some help. They are not as good health as they have been and will need some help soon.

We love the guest bedroom at Davie and Jennifer's fixed for us, but having our place would be even better.

Evelyn said, "Bobby loved growing up here in this house. It is a lovely and wonderful place to live.

Bobby said, "We have discussed buying it if you ever decide to sell it. I think your plan to relocate to Linkersville is good."

Eve said, "Bobby, if you are still interested in buying this place, I am all for us doing that."

Bobby hugged his wife and said, "Thanks, Evelyn."

Turning to his mom and dad, he said, "We are still interested in buying your home when you decide to sell it. Our duplex has been great, but we do not have a lot of space for the future."

Several days later, Jennifer missed her grandparents and asked the kids if they would like to visit their great-grandpa and great-grandma.

They said, "Yes, Mom, we love to go to their house. Great Grandpa Charlie is so much fun. We love spending time with them.

Jenny said, "Great Grandma shows me things I can make in her kitchen. I help her cook things."

Jennifer called her grandmother to ask if they would like company for a few days.

They said, "Yes, we would love having you come over and bring those precious children."

She called Davie and told him there were plans to spend a few days with her grandparents. He was thrilled she wanted to visit and spend time with them.

He knew the kids would love being there. He told her he would join them after he got off from work.

She said, "Great, and I look forward to spending time with them, and you are joining us in the evenings."

When Jennifer arrived at her grandparents' house, Jenny and Jimmy were out of the car the minute they arrived.

Grandpa Charlie greeted Jennifer and the children with big hugs.

Grandma Irene came out on the porch, hugged them all, and said, "I have some cookies fresh from an oven that needs to be eaten. Does anyone want to help me eat those cookies?"

Everyone headed to the kitchen. Jennifer got the kids some milk to go with their cookies and some milk so she could join them in eating cookies. Her grandmother made the best cookies.

Irene sat there watching them all and, looking over at Jennifer, was pleased to see a look of peace and tranquility on her face.

Grandma Irene said, "Jennifer, you seem to have found some peace and tranquility, and I am so glad. You have been through so much but have found the strength to move beyond all that has occurred.

I have prayed consistently for you and your beautiful family."

Jennifer said, "Grandma, I adore and look up to you. You have been there for me in every event in my life, and the Spiritual wisdom you expressed to me when I needed it the most.

Thank you for reminding me that prayer, faith, and allowing God to help me would help me overcome some of those terrible events.

You reminded me that with God, all things are possible. You also encouraged me to put God first in my life. Davie and I are attending church faithfully now and look forward to each Sunday.

We are going to the church you and Grandpa attended all those years and where Davie went. The kids are excited about going to church every Sunday."

Grandpa showed up in the kitchen and said, "When you finish the cookies, I was wondering if I could get some help hooking up the horse to that old wagon outside.

I thought we might go on a trip through the woods. I know where to stand on the ridge and see the valley below."

Grandma Irene asked, "Jennifer, will we stay here and let them have all the fun?"

Jennifer said, "No, Grandma, there is enough room in that wagon for us, too, so let's go with them."

Grandma packed a few things in a bag to eat and some water in a jug in case someone got hungry or thirsty. She also took a blanket if it got cooler when they returned home this evening.

They all loaded into the wagon, and Jimmy got to help Grandpa hook up the horse to the wagon. They loved the ride through the woods.

Jimmy spotted birds up in the trees. Jenny saw some pretty flowers in the woods and wanted to stop and pick some.

Grandpa stopped and helped her down from the wagon. She picked several different flowers. She returned to the wagon, and Grandpa helped her back in the wagon.

She gave half of them to her Great-Grandma and the other flowers to her mom and hugged them each.

Jimmy saw a big squirrel run up the tree and showed it to his sister. She smiled and said, "Jimmy, he climbed up the tree fast."

Grandpa Charlie came to the place where he had always loved to take his sweetheart Irene. He helped Irene and Jennifer down from the wagon.

Then he told Jimmy, "I want you to help me get your little sister down. I will be here to assist if you need me."

Jimmy said, "Okay, I can help you."

Jimmy reached out to his sister, and she stepped down from the wagon. Jimmy caught her and set her on the ground with a big grin.

Jimmy and Jenny took off running through the valley.

Charlie smiled and thought of all the times he had come here with Irene. She walked over to him. He reached out and hugged her and thanked her for being there with him all those years.

She smiled and said, "Charlie, we have been through some tough times, but here we are now, with our family and sharing our beautiful valley with them.

God has been good to us and given us all these years together. I thank God for you every day.

We seldom hear from Terry. We know he loves us, and we have accepted his life is much different than what he had here with us.

Tom's wife, Peggy, is the daughter we never had. So glad they are thinking about moving back here."

Looking over at Jennifer, they saw their beautiful granddaughter looking more at peace than they had seen her in a while."

Jennifer turned and saw her grandpa and grandma with their arms around each other, and she smiled.

They had inspired her and were a spiritual source of guidance and help. She joined them and hugged them both.

What a peaceful and wonderful place here. She had memories of her and Bobby coming here in the winter and sliding down that hill into the valley on their sleds.

Grandma had brought a snack, so Charlie called the kids to return to the top of the mountain so that they could eat. He wanted to start back soon before it got dark.

They ate their snack and loaded it back up in the wagon. No one wanted to leave, but they knew great grandpa was right.

On their return to the house, Charlie heard a loud noise and felt the wagon jerk to one side. Everyone exited the wagon, and Charlie checked to see what had happened.

The wooden wagon wheel had run over a rock in the tall grass, and it was enough to bust the wagon wheel. Charlie could tell the wheel was beyond repair. The wagon and those wheels were old.

No one could walk back to the house because of the distance, and it would be dark soon.

Charlie looked for something to support and brace the wagon where the wheel had broken. They would sleep in the wagon tonight.

Jennifer saw a stump near the wagon and asked her grandpa if they could slide the wagon over onto the stump. It was the right height to brace the wagon.

Charlie knew it would work if they found something they could use to raise the wagon and push it over on the stump.

Disconnecting the horse from the wagon, he knew the single tree used to hook the horse to the wagon would be strong. It would give him some leverage.

Charlie said, "When I use this single tree for leverage, I want you to all push the wagon over to the side."

Everyone got on one side of the wagon, ready to push when he told them. Even Jimmy and Jenny were trying to help.

Irene knew she was still in decent shape for her age. She was concerned about Jennifer's condition and strength soon after being raped.

Charlie said, "Push! Everyone pushed, and the back of the wagon moved to one side.

Charlie said, "Stop now; you have done an excellent job. The back of the wagon is resting on top of the stump."

Jennifer felt the strain of pushing and some pain, but she was okay.

It was not dark yet, but it would be soon. Irene knew of a small creek where they could get some water to drink. It was from a natural stream with pure water and was okay for drinking. They all followed her through the woods to the stream of water.

Jimmy broke limbs on the path so he would not get lost. Charlie grinned because he remembered telling Jimmy how to avoid getting lost in the woods.

Irene kneeled by the creek and cupped her hands to form a cup to drink from. They all joined her and kneeled to drink the water. It tasted so good.

Charlie grinned when they started back to the wagon, and Jimmy showed him the way back with his broken limbs.

When they reached the wagon, Charlie told Jimmy they would gather pine needles and put them in the back. This would be soft to lie on and help to keep them warm.

The sun had gone down. It was getting dark, so they all loaded into the back of the wagon. They used the blanket Irene had brought to cover them up.

Jennifer lay there remembering when she had visited them one Christmas, and her grandpa had gone to the barn to milk the cows.

It was snowing badly, but he knew the cows needed to be milked. When he did not return, her grandma was getting concerned. Her grandma would go out into the snowstorm to see if he was okay.

She knew her grandma was strong but did not need to be in that weather.

Jennifer wore her snowmobile suit and boots and pulled the hood over her head. Her grandma gave her a lantern to help her see in the blinding snow. She told her she would set a light in the window that would help to guide her back to the house.

When she found her grandpa buried in a snow drift and unconscious, she knew he would need medical help. She had returned to the house, kicking snow aside as she walked to find the path back to him.

Arriving at the house, her grandma tried to call for help, but the phones were dead. Jennifer knew it was up to her to save her grandpa's life.

She found an old Army cot she could use to put her grandpa on and then drag him to the house. It was the hardest thing she had ever done when she got him onto the cot and him unconscious.

Dragging him in the heavy snow seemed almost impossible. She made it to the house but said several prayers for God to help her pull him to the house. She had made it there, and that event helped her realize she needed to change her life. She had become rebellious and resentful.

She prayed that she and her grandfather made it back to the house in a snowstorm.

Her grandpa regained consciousness and later was taken by their neighbor Jerry on a snowmobile to the hospital.

Now, they were stranded in the woods, and Jennifer knew God would watch over them. And when Davie got to her grandparent's house, and no one was there, he would know something must be wrong and try to find them.

They were all snuggled together in the wagon. It helped them stay warm, being so close to each other, and the pine needles made it a soft place to rest for the night or until they were found.

Davie arrived at Charlie's place and walked inside; no one was there. There were no lights on, and nothing cooked in the kitchen. He was deeply concerned.

Jennifer's car was still in the driveway. He walked out to the garage, and the truck and Irene's car were there.

He walked down to the barn. The cows had not been milked. He saw the old wagon was missing, and the horse was not in the barn or the lot.

He milked the cows for Charlie, knowing he liked those cows milked every day. Taking the milk back to the house, he took his phone out, called Chief Roberts, and told him he might need help at Charlie and Irene's place.

He explained that Jennifer and the kids were here visiting with them. No one is home; the only thing missing is Charlie's wagon and horse.

He said, "I figured Charlie took them all for a ride in the wagon through the woods. Unfortunately, something must have happened because the sun is falling, and they are not back.

I know Charlie would not have kept them out this late."

The Chief told him he would send some officers to help and set up a rescue squad.

The officers arrived and had a 4-wheeler on a trailer. They began by following a trail. Davie knew that trail led them to a big open meadow through the woods.

They could see wagon wheel tracks, so they knew they were headed in the right direction. Davie was using a spotlight to help light the pathway.

They had brought a blanket, some hot chocolate, and coffee, knowing that when they found them, they would be cold from being out this late at night.

They spotted the wagon and the horse tied to a tree up ahead. Davie called out to them to see if anyone was near the wagon.

The wagon was being held up on one side with it braced on a stump, and inside that wagon were the ones they were looking for.

The lights and noise awaken them, and they raised to see Davie and a few officers standing at the wagon's side.

Jimmy said, "Dad, is that you?"

Davie said, "Yes, son, it is me. So glad to see you are all okay."

The officers helped Davie get everyone out of the wagon.

Davie was not surprised to see pine needles in the wagon. He had spent much time with Charlie as a boy, and Charlie had taught him a lot during those times.

Charlie told him there was another wagon wheel in the barn, but it had been too late to try to walk back to the house and get the wagon wheel.

He was not sure any of them were able to walk that distance.

Two officers said they would follow the trail back to the house and get the wheel.

Irene, Jennifer, and the kids could not walk that far tonight.

Davie told them where to find things in the barn for the wagon. Davie and one of the other officers waited with them at the wagon.

They had brought some extra blankets and gave them the thermos of coffee and hot chocolate. They had brought some paper cups to drink the coffee and hot chocolate.

The two men found the wheel and tools needed and noticed the 4-wheeler there. They found the key for it and rode it back. Two 4-wheelers would be nice tonight to help get everyone back home.

Davie heard the 4-wheelers coming down the path. Everyone got out of the wagon with help from one of the officers. The other officers got the broken wheel off and the other wheel back on the wagon.

They had moved it off the stump. They had a jack they brought to hold the wagon up while they changed the wheels.

Davie got the horse and hooked it back up to the wagon. The horse got excited when the officer started up the 4-wheeler. Charlie calmed the horse down by talking to his horse.

Two of the lights they brought were mounted to the wagon so they could see the path. Davie sat on the bench beside Charlie to help him see the pathway back.

The officers on the two 4-wheelers were just up ahead of the wagon. The other two officers followed the wagon back to the house.

Irene insisted the officers come inside and warm up when they arrived at the house. She set a big platter of cookies down on the table and had hot chocolate and hot coffee ready for them to drink in no time.

The kids enjoyed the cookies and milk. After they finished the cookies and milk, Davie took them upstairs and tucked them into their beds for the night.

Jennifer was worn out and had gone upstairs, also. Davie checked on her and kissed her goodnight.

He wanted to go back downstairs and thank the officers for their help. She nodded okay and went to sleep.

Davie rejoined the officers downstairs. He told them how much he appreciated their help and thanked them.

Charlie and Irene had also gone to bed. They were very tired. Davie noticed how extremely tired Charlie was, but it had been a very tough night for Charlie. He had done an excellent job of caring for his family.

Davie walked outside with the officers when they finished their coffee and cookies. He knew they had to report to work the next morning and had sacrificed their sleep to help find Charlie and everyone tonight.

Davie and the other officers had told the Chief that the lost had been found. The Chief told them all to come in later in the morning. The night crew had offered to work longer so the men could get some rest and come in two hours later for the day shift.

Davie cleaned up the kitchen after everyone had left.

When he went upstairs, he checked on the kids, who slept soundly in bed. He got ready for bed and noticed Jennifer looked so peaceful lying there in the bed.

Davie woke up the next morning to the smell of coffee and bacon. He dressed and went downstairs to have breakfast.

Irene had a big breakfast ready for them. She knew they had missed supper the night before, so they would be hungry. She also had pancake mix ready to make pancakes.

Irene and Charlie were in a deep conversation. Irene got him some coffee.

Davie sat down at the table and ate a big breakfast.

Charlie said, "Davie, I was glad to see the rescue squad last night.

The kids and Jennifer enjoyed our trip to the meadow in the woods. When we returned to the house, Irene told them about a natural spring in the woods. Jimmy showed me how he marked the trail so we would not get lost going back to the wagon.

We loaded back into the wagon to head home. There was a rock hidden in the tall grass along the trail. The wagon hit the rock exactly right, and it busted the wheel.

I knew we were stranded for the night. I knew it was too far to walk and would be dark soon. Jimmy helped me fill up the wagon with pine needles.

You and Jennifer have some good kids. You have done an excellent job as a parent.

I was glad to see Jennifer more relaxed; she will be okay. She has been through a lot.

Our granddaughter has always been such a joy and grandson also. He was like Tom in many ways. Now we are enjoying these great-grandkids." The footsteps coming down the stairway meant the kids were awake and hungry.

Irene was already at the stove getting ready to fill up their plates.

Davie went upstairs to check on Jennifer. She was awake when he entered the room.

Jennifer said, "Davie, I am gaining ground emotionally but still tender, sore from the rape and loss of a baby. I know the doctors had to make many repairs inside me where I had been brutally raped.

I thought I would be physically okay, but it will take longer to completely heal the body. I am thankful I am alive and here with all of you.

I will always miss our baby girl, and I am sad that we will never have any more children, but thankful for the two wonderful kids God blessed us with."

Tears came into her eyes, and Davie held her close to him. He also had tears in his eyes for the baby girl the rapist took away from them.

They joined the family downstairs, and Jennifer ate some of her grandmother's pancakes. Irene knew how much Jennifer loved her pancakes.

Davie, Jennifer, and the children left later that morning and returned to their house.

Jennifer was glad she and the kids had gone on their trip through the woods. They had enjoyed their time with her grandparents.

After they left, Charlie said, "Irene, it was great having the family here. I hate that the old wagon wheel broke. I know that old wagon is like me, and it is old. I know the kids enjoyed the trip yesterday, but we were tired.

I am glad they had an enjoyable time. It reminded me of when I took Jennifer and Bobby in the old wagon. It was nice being there with you, Irene, in the woods.

It reminded me of the past when we used to go there. We are getting older and unsure how much longer we will be able to enjoy our farm."

The next morning, Charlie milked the cows and gathered the eggs. He made sure the stock was all okay and headed to the house. He felt extremely tired and thought he would take a nap this morning.

Irene heard him come back inside and found him in the easy chair he loved to sit in.

She noticed the color on his face was not good and asked him if he felt okay. He told her he was only tired and was going to take a nap.

He went to sleep, and she sat in her chair near him. He had mentioned before he went to the barn that he had some indigestion.

He thought it was from missing supper the night before and eating too many cookies before bed.

She had been concerned about his messing with the wagon when the wooden tire was broken the day before. She knew he had lifted a lot of weight when he lifted the wagon. He seemed okay, though, afterward.

She noticed his breathing had changed while he was asleep. He woke up and looked straight at her.

Charlie said, "Irene, I do not feel particularly good now. For some reason, my chest is also hurting. I will be okay. I think I will not do much today and just rest."

Irene wondered if he might be having some heart issues. She knew he had some heart problems.

Irene picked up the phone and called their doctor. She told him how Charlie was feeling and what she was seeing. He told her to call an ambulance and get him to the hospital, and he would meet them there.

Later, Irene called Tom to let him know she was at the hospital with Charlie. She called the heart doctor, who told her to get an ambulance and take Charlie to the hospital.

When Tom hung up the phone, he told Irene to get things ready to go to Linkersville because they had taken his dad to the hospital with a heart attack.

Peggy said, "I will pack some things quickly and be ready to go shortly."

Tom called Jennifer and Davie while she packed and told them about Charlie and his being taken to the hospital.

Davie was glad he was there when Jennifer got the news because she was in tears. She loved her grandpa and did not want anything to happen to him.

They left for the hospital as soon as Davie hung up the phone. Davie dropped the kids off at his mom and dad. He told them to pray for Charlie. He told them he was unsure how long they would be at the hospital.

His mom and dad told him they would care for those grandkids and not to worry, and they would be praying for all of them, especially for Charlie and Irene.

Arriving at the hospital, they let Jennifer and Davie see Charlie for a few minutes, then took him to ICU-CCU.

Grandma Irene was in tears as they pushed his cart down the hall and into the elevator. The paramedics had let her ride in the ambulance with them. They knew about Charlie's previous heart issues.

Irene was waiting in the waiting room and, turning around, saw Jennifer running toward her in the waiting area. They both had a good cry.

Grandma Irene assured Charlie that he was well cared for and God would take care of him. If this was his time to go to heaven, then she knew God knew this was best for Charlie.

Jennifer sat beside her grandmother, and Davie was on the other side. They held her hands, and they were all in tears.

Tom and Peggy arrived at the hospital not long after the call. He was glad to see his mom was not alone.

Jennifer, Davie, and Grandma Irene saw Tom and Peggy and went to them. They were all in tears again but so glad they were there together and eager to see Charlie again.

The doctor came out and said, "Charlie's condition is not good, but we have been able to stabilize him. You can all go in for only a few minutes, but I know Tom, you have not seen your dad yet, so Irene, you can go first with Tom and Peggy.

Charlie was proud to see his family there and knew he was not doing well. He was proud his son was moving back here. He knew his sweet wife would be well cared for by their son Tom, Peggy, and the rest of the family.

Charlie looked at his son and said, "Tom, I know I can count on you and Peggy to be here for Irene while I am in the hospital."

Charlie said, "Glad you are planning to return here to live, son. My old heart is worn out. Not sure how much longer the ole heart is going to last."

Tom said, "Dad, thanks for what you said, and "Yes," we will be moving back here. Bobby and Eve are buying our home so that we will move here soon."

Irene said, "Charlie, you get your rest. You know God is watching over you, and you are in a good hospital. You are being well cared for in this hospital. I am okay because I have family here and God to give me what I need."

The nurse said their time to visit was up. They gave Charlie their hugs and a kiss on his cheek and told him they would be out in the waiting area. Peggy also kissed him on the cheek and said, "Charlie, you are in good hands, and we love you."

Jennifer and Davie got to see Charlie for only a few moments. They saw Charlie's eyes light up when he saw them again.

Jennifer hugged him and said, "Grandpa, I love you so much, and you are the best grandpa in the world. I will also be praying for you."

Charlie nodded, and the nurse noticed he seemed distressed and asked them to leave.

The doctor left Charlie's room and walked into the waiting area to speak with the family.

He said, "Charlie has stabilized again. His heart is not strong. He tires easily, but the visit from his loved ones also makes him feel better. We must continue to limit the time spent with him for now."

Irene said, "Dr. Stanley, you have cared for both of us for many years.

As you know, God is also there caring for him, and we have put our faith in God and you as our wonderful doctor.

We know you will do whatever you can for Charlie. We will be here praying for him and you, Dr. Stanley."

The doctor left them with tears. He took a few moments to regain his composure and returned to Charlie's room.

He had known this family for a lot of years. He also realized that Charlie might not have much longer to live, but he was grateful to spend a little time with those he loved before he was taken to heaven.

Tom had called his brother to let him know about their dad. Terry said he could not come then but to tell his mom and dad he loved them.

Charlie passed away that evening.

As he drew his last breath, the doctor allowed the family to be with him. Irene had been holding his hand. He had squeezed her hand and, in a whisper, told Irene, "Love you honey, and see you on the other side, and went to be with the Lord." The angels had come to take him to his heavenly home. They left the hospital.

Tom and their family returned to the home Tom had loved so much all those years he was growing up. It would not be the same for his mom and any of them without Charlie.

Word got out quickly about Charlie passing away. The next day, neighbors and friends came and brought food and words of love for the family.

Davie's mom and dad brought the grandkids with them to visit Irene. Davie had asked them to bring the kids. Davie and Jennifer were so glad they did.

Jerry and Marilyn had told them that Great-grandpa Charlie had gone to heaven to be with God before they visited with Irene.

When the grandkids arrived, Jimmy hugged his mom and said, "Mom, great-grandpa is sure in a wonderful place we know they call heaven.

Someday, we will get to be with him there. We will miss him, but he will be busy with God and Jesus in heaven."

Jenny just cried and said, "I loved him too, but Jimmy is right about heaven being a wonderful place to go. I am glad Great Gran is here. We can help take care of her."

The funeral was special, with words of comfort from their pastor to them and others who had attended. His words from the bible

were also comforting. He shared a lot of good times he had enjoyed with Irene and Charlie over the years.

Terry and their family had come for the funeral. They stayed in a motel the night before and left after the services ended.

There were many things to do later that month after Charlie's funeral. Tom and his family took care of things.

Irene told them she wanted to talk to them when they had some quiet time. She knew they were planning to return here and buy a home. They gathered around the table.

Irene said, "Tom and Peggy, how would you feel about buying this place instead of some home nearby? I know I will be okay for a while, but should I need help, it would be good knowing you are here.

How do you feel about buying this place and me staying here in this home for a while longer?"

Tom looked at his mom and looked at Peggy and smiled. They had been talking about staying there with his mom while they looked for a place to buy nearby.

Tom knew the "Will" stated he and Terry would be the beneficiary. If he bought the place, he would give Terry his half and live here.

They told Irene that if she wanted to sell it right now, they would buy it from her and give Terry his half of this inheritance. Tom also told her he loved being back here and living here.

Irene went with them to their lawyer. He drew the papers so Tom and Peggy could purchase his parent's home. He also made provisions for Terry to get his half when the bank approved the loan for Tom to purchase the home.

Irene was given a lifetime right to live there in the home. She loved the arrangements and looked forward to having them move into the house that would be theirs.

CHAPTER 8

Moving Time

Tom hired an attorney to manage all the paperwork regarding selling his home in Rosewood.

The purchase of his mom and dad's home in Linkersville involved paying his brother what he had inherited.

His brother had no interest in his parent's place or land. He only wanted his portion of the inheritance. Using an attorney would ensure that everything is done legally.

Tom was buying his mom and dad's place because he wanted to move back home to be there for his mother. Buying the place would make it possible to keep his mom in her home.

Peggy started boxing up things she wanted to move to Linkersville. It was amazing how many things you collected and kept over the years. She packed and sorted out things she thought Bobby and Evelyn might want or need.

They did not plan to take very much furniture because Tom's mom had a house full of beautiful furniture that belonged in that house.

Charlie and Irene had lots of money when they came here to live. He built her their beautiful home himself. He had built a home to last for many years. The house was still in great shape for its age.

Irene was thrilled Tom and Peggy were moving back. She loved those two and missed seeing them as often as she would have liked.

When Charlie passed away, she was fearful she would have to leave her home and live in a nursing home.

Tom wanted her to stay in her home. He knew if he bought the place, no one could move her out of her home.

Tom had always been so thoughtful and caring. He was a lot like his dad.

The bank had approved Tom and Peggy's loan. The money was split two ways. Tom had a check made out from the bank for his brother. After the loan was approved, the new title was made out in Tom's and Peggy's names.

His mother had inherited financial security when Charlie died. Charlie knew Irene could not care for the place by herself.

He had been thrilled before he died, knowing Tom and Peggy would be living there and owning the home, and his sweetheart Irene would be cared for by his oldest son, Tom.

Peggy was thrilled they got a lawyer to manage everything. Tom's brother, Terry, called to let Tom know he received the check, his part of the sale of his parent's homeplace.

Terry was nothing like Tom, Charlie, or anyone she had ever met in the family. He had a unique personality and preferred living where he was, which was fine because his wife also preferred living there.

He told Tom that he would never have been contented living in Linkersville.

Now, all she and Tom had to do was go home and pack some more stuff.

Peggy had always loved Tom's parent's beautiful home and land. It was great going there to visit. They would have never found a place to buy that would bring them the joy they would receive from owning and living in Charlie and Irene's home.

Bobby and Evelyn were thrilled when they got their title to his parent's home. He loved growing up in this house. Now, he and Evelyn could make their memories here.

They did not have much to move from the Duplex where they had lived for several years. Maybe someday, I will even have little ones to raise here.

Peggy and Tom made several trips to Linkerville with things she had already packed. Irene was thrilled each time they moved their things to Linkerville.

Now that the house's title was in their name, they could plan to move everything. She knew Bobby and Evelyn were also eager to get moved.

Evelyn was thrilled when Peggy told her they would leave the dining room furniture for them if they wanted the dining room furniture. Irene had a beautiful table in her dining room they gave them.

Peggy also gave them a set of dishes she had kept for many years. Evelyn was thrilled. They were beautiful dishes, and she enjoyed using them.

When they brought a few things to the farm, they spent some time with his mom and shared some of the items they were bringing with her. She offered to pack up or get rid of some of her things.

Peggy said, "We are not bringing all our things from Rosewood. Bobby and his wife lived in a furnished duplex, so they did not have much furniture. They are thrilled to be getting much of our furniture we will not need here.

I have some pictures to put on the wall in the living room that I plan to bring. All your pictures will remain on the walls. I plan to re-arrange the pictures." Irene was in tears knowing her son and Peggy would be living here, which brought her joy.

Tom had always liked living here when he was a boy. He was so much help to his dad when he was growing up. Terry never liked being on the farm and was glad when he could move away.

Tom said, "Mom, Peggy, and I borrowed enough money to add a master bedroom for us on the back of the house.

We want to be downstairs with you. The kids and grandkids can have those bedrooms upstairs when they visit."

Irene said, "Tom, that is a wonderful plan. I am thrilled you are both going to be here from now on. I do not have many years left, but living in this home means a lot. Having you here means even more to me."

Tom left the room to make some calls. He knew Jerry was a great carpenter, and they could build much of the room themselves like they did to help Davie and Jennifer with the bedroom they both helped build.

Jerry was thrilled Tom and Peggy were moving back here. He said he would be over in the morning to help him sketch the layout and plan.

Tom said, "That is great, and see you in the morning."

Tom told Peggy and his mom that Jerry would arrive later this morning. He will draw up plans for adding this master bedroom for us to this house. I enjoy working with Jerry. He is a good carpenter and can build about anything."

Hearing a truck outside, Tom went to the door. It was Jerry, and he had brought some tools with him. Jerry came inside and spoke to Peggy and Irene. Tom and Jerry went outside to see what needed to be done to add the room.

Jerry thought where they wanted the room was a good place to add it to the house.

Returning, they sat at the table and laid out the blueprint and plans. It was going to be a nice addition.

Jerry and Tom also checked inside the house, where they would make the door to the bedroom.

Jerry said, "Tom, we have enough time today to dig a trench for the foundation. I brought some shovels, and we can use them today.

I figure Charlie has some shovels and other tools out in his garage. When we take a break, we will check later and see what other tools he has out there we might need."

The next morning, when Jerry arrived, a concrete truck arrived with the concrete they needed for the foundation. They had framed in the trench for the foundation. After the concrete had been poured, Tom and Jerry smoothed off the top of the concrete. After the concrete dried well, they could start laying the concrete blocks.

Irene and Peggy ensured they had some things to eat when they took a break from working.

The rest of the week was spent getting lumber and things that needed to be ordered and delivered. They worked in Charlie's garage building the rafters.

Charlie had the tools they needed. He had done lots of carpenter work over the years.

Jerry got a hold of the contractors who had done the work on Davie and Jennifer's bedroom. He did excellent work and was reasonable, considering the cost of labor to add a room to the house.

The concrete mortar for the blocks for the foundation was dry now, and the blocks were laid for the foundation of the room to be built. The workers were ready to start putting up walls and rafters.

Irene remembered those years Charlie used to do carpenter work on their house. He would surely love what they were doing now with that addition. They had talked about building another bedroom downstairs but never felt it was needed then.

Irene was glad Tom and Peggy would be sleeping downstairs near where she slept. They were so thoughtful and caring.

Davie and Bobby joined Tom and Jerry in the work at Charlie and Irene's home. Building the bedroom onto the house would be nice for Tom and Peggy when they move into the house.

After Charlie passed away, Tom wanted to be close to his mom to care for her when she needed help.

His mom was thrilled Tom bought the house. She knew he would take diligent care of the house and farm. She was pleased to see all the help Tom had in building this room onto what is now his house.

Tom was grateful for all the help he was getting. He hoped they could finish the work and then move into the house. With all this help, the work was being done much quicker than he thought it would take.

Irene and Peggy drove to town. Irene was enjoying being out with Peggy today. She loved her daughter-in-law, and they had always been remarkably close.

Peggy had been so good to Tom and her and Charlie. They always got along great. She had seemed more like a daughter than a daughter-in-law.

Peggy bought a walk-in shower and a square tub. It was the perfect size for the new bathroom. They also found a vanity and the sinks she wanted. The tile was the next thing they looked for.

Irene found something she thought Peggy might like. When Peggy saw it, she said, "Yes, Irene, that is exactly what I was looking for."

Peggy did not want Irene to get too tired, so they took a break and ate lunch.

After lunch, they found a few more things Peggy wanted to pick up while she was in town.

Later that day, the delivery truck brought the vanity and other things she had purchased. Bobby and Davie helped unload the things they had purchased for the bathroom.

They stored those on her porch, out of the way of the men working in the bathroom.

Jennifer brought Jimmy and Jenny to her grandparents' home after they woke up from naps.

It did not seem right for her grandfather to not be there. Knowing her mom and dad had bought the house and would be moving into her grandparents' house was great. She was thrilled to have them close by and now with her grandmother.

Jennifer was shocked to see how much work they had done on the room. The new room was framed and covered outside with siding, and the roofing was done. The men were working now on the inside doing the drywall. They had mudding to do on the seams of the drywall and wooden frame.

Grandma Irene and Peggy made sure there was plenty to eat when they got hungry.

Earlier in the week, her grandma told her that Tom and Jerry had done all the work on the room's foundation.

They did not even need the contractors to come and work. They put up the framing for the walls and, with your grandpa's tractor, could put the rafter they had made up on top of the framing.

Grandma said, "Your grandpa would have been so proud of the things they did. Your grandpa had all the tools they needed. They also had help from Davie and Bobby."

I miss Charlie so much, but I am so happy Tom and Peggy bought this place and want me to stay home.

They built that room so they would be downstairs with me if I needed them during the night.

Jennifer, having a family that loves and cares about you is great. I was proud they were there for you recently when you were going through a rough time.

There will be tough days ahead, but with a loving and caring family and God up above, you will be okay.

Always look to God and God's word, the bible, for help. Remember this scripture in John 16:33 that says, "These things I have spoken unto you, that in me you might have peace. In the world ye shall have tribulations: but be of good cheer; I have overcome the world."

Grandma Irene hugged her and reminded her that some of us are getting older, and we will go to be with God like our grandpa did with the Lord.

During our lifetime here, we have tried to give each of our children, families, grandchildren, and great-grandchildren love and support in whatever way we could.

Jennifer hugged her grandmother again and knew she had improved because of her grandparent's love and spiritual support.

Next week, they would work on the plumbing. The electrician had come out several weeks ago. He wired the bathroom and ran the wiring to the main circuit box. The main plumbing had been done before the drywall was put up. They only had to hook up the tub, shower, vanity, and commode.

The following morning, Grandma Irene fixed a big breakfast for everyone. They had also invited the plumber and electrician to come and join them for breakfast.

Everyone knew Irene was an exceptionally good cook. Peggy had helped Irene, and they had a great breakfast of pancakes, fried eggs, scrambled eggs, bacon, sausage, biscuits, and homemade gravy.

After breakfast, Tom and Bobby installed the doorway and hung the door. The vanity, tub, shower, and commode were installed and hooked to the plumbing.

Jerry and Bobby were putting the tile around the sink. The tile for the floor would be done last.

Everything was done but the floors and the walls in the bathroom. They planned to finish those things next week. They were hopeful they would be moved into the house by the weekend.

Irene told Peggy, "I cannot believe how much work they did in such a short time. I thought this might take months."

The men laid down their tools to join Irene and Peggy. They found the dining table full of food. They sat down and ate. Jerry said the grace before they ate. He thanked God for blessing them with strength and the ability to construct this addition and for those who took the time to help them. He thanked God for Irene and Peggy and the healthy food.

The next week, Tom and Jerry finished the work that was needed. After the drywalls were finished, they painted the bathroom and bedroom.

They both put down the pad and carpeting in the bedroom. The last job was putting the tiles down in the bathroom.

Standing back and looking at the two rooms, they bowed their heads and thanked God for health, strength, and Davie and Bobby helping them.

Both agreed that contractors were not needed when they discovered all the carpenter tools put away in the cabinets in the garage, which they could use for building the room onto the house.

Charlie had built the house himself when he and Irene first got married.

Tom said, "When he needed a helper, he would get some of his family who had also come to the United States, and Uncle Joe to help him.

That evening, they invited Davie, Bobby, and Evelyn to come and join them for supper.

When the meal was over, they let everyone see the finished rooms. Peggy had seen it in the earlier stages of building the room. She stood amazed at how nice it was and how large the bathroom and bedroom were. Everyone was amazed at them getting it done so quickly and how nice it looked.

The plans for the weekend included everyone taking a truck and pulling trailers, going to Rosewood, and moving their things from Rosewood to Linkerville.

For Tom, it was truly going back home. He had grown up in that house, which had many good memories. Now, it was his home, including him, Peggy, and his precious mom.

Peggy had left Friday to ensure things were ready in their house to move things to Linkersville. She had put tags on the things to leave for Bobby and Evelyn.

Everyone arrived early and started loading trucks and trailers. Peggy was thankful she had packed things earlier in the month, so it was ready to be moved.

Marilyn called Jennifer and told her she would come to their house and take care of the grandkids so she could be at her grandma's and mom and dad's house in Linkerville when the trucks arrived to unload her parent's things.

Eve helped Peggy clean up the house after the trucks and trailers pulled away and left for Linkersville. Peggy did not want to leave much cleaning for them to do later.

She knew Eve and Bobby would make their memories in this house, and a few tears trickled down her face as she thought of all the memories from the past.

Peggy knew she would miss this place but was glad to visit Bobby and Eve. This would be a lovely home for them. They were excited about owning their own home. Bobby was returning to the home he grew up in, and Tom was returning to the home he grew up in.

Peggy hugged Eve and said, "You are a wonderful wife for Bobby. He is so blessed to have you in his life. I know you will enjoy living here and raising your family here."

Eve turned back to cleaning some in the kitchen. Looking out the window, she was eager to see the doctor next week. There was a good chance she was pregnant.

She had not told Bobby yet that she thought she was pregnant. She was careful not to do anything foolish that might cause her to have a miscarriage. The men had moved all the heavy things and boxes.

Eve wanted to tell the future father on their first night in their home. Her doctor's appointment was tomorrow morning.

She knew the family would be pleased. Bobby will be a wonderful dad. He loves kids and has wanted to have children to love and care for.

Eve wanted children also but had been told she would never be able to have children. Grandma Irene had been preparing some things to eat while the family was busy getting Tom and Peggy's things into the house. She had fixed things that could be eaten whenever they wanted to stop and eat.

After cleaning at Rosewood, Eve rode with Peggy back to Linkersville. Tom and Davie told Bobby they would help him move some things from the duplex when he was ready.

Bobby said, "I do not have any furniture to move because the duplex was furnished. Mostly, it is dishes, clothes, and small items.

Some of those things we have already moved to the house. If I see I need any help, I will let you know. I have a truck, so moving should be easy.

When their clothes were brought in, Peggy had them lay the clothes on the bed. She knew she could hang those things up later and put away the other things in their new dresser and chest.

By nighttime, Peggy had put away the clothes and had the bed ready to sleep in tonight.

She loved the color of paint she had chosen for their bedroom and bathroom. The towels were in the built-in cabinet in the bathroom.

The bath rugs were on the floors. Standing back and cooking in the room, she was so pleased with how nice the bathroom and bedroom looked and would be spending their first night in their new bedroom.

Jennifer and Eve joined Irene in the kitchen. Peggy finished showing the men where to put the furniture in the living room.

Most of the boxes were left on the porch for the time being. Boxes marked kitchen were taken to the kitchen.

Peggy joined them in the kitchen, and they began to unload the boxes. Peggy and Irene had already cleared some shelves for most of the things in the boxes. They put those things away and got rid of the boxes.

Peggy said, "Irene, we should take a break."

Irene said, "Yes, I think I am getting tired, so let's take something to drink and go back on the porch."

Finding places to sit down, they rested some and enjoyed their iced tea.

Irene said, "I sure do miss Charlie, but I am thankful I have you here. I have loved you all these years, and you have loved me in return.

I look forward to being with you for several more years before I am with my Lord and Charlie.

This home has brought so much joy and happiness, and what a blessing to know my family will continue to enjoy this now and even when I am gone.

We will have a wonderful time together for as long as God permits me to stay here. So glad we can share this time."

Jennifer hugged her grandma and told her she loved her. Eve hugged her, too, and said she loved being a part of this family. She told Grandma Irene, "Not only do I love you, but I also respect you for being the wonderful, loving, and caring person we all love.

I love the close relationship you have with God. You are an inspiration to all of us."

Peggy got up from her chair with tears in her eyes. She said, "Irene, I am thrilled we will be here for you and our memories of Charlie.

You both were wonderful parents to your sons and loved so much by your grandchildren. Tom is so blessed to have you for his mother and all those years he spent with his dad.

I have loved you since the day I met you. You were kind and so good to me and made me feel like a part of the family.

Thank you for letting us buy the house so we can live here and care for this home and farm for many more years and enjoy having you with us. You could have kept the house in your name for the years you lived here. You chose instead to let us buy the house. Thanks for allowing us to sell ours and buy this beautiful home."

It was getting late, and everyone was tired, so Bobby and Eve left for Rosewood.

Jennifer and Davie drove back to their place.

Jerry went home so he could take a shower. He knew Marilyn would be back there soon.

He was proud she could spend time with the grandkids and Jennifer could be there when they arrived with the trucks and trailer.

Irene was getting tired. Peggy told her she would finish in the kitchen.

Irene said, "Okay, I will shower and go to bed early tonight."

Peggy had the kitchen clean in no time. She found Tom sitting in his favorite chair. He smiled at her as she walked into the room.

He said, "Peggy, I am tired. How about we go to bed early in our new bedroom."

Tom loved his new walk-in shower. They had a large showerhead over the tub where they used to live. His large shower was great.

Peggy got into the new whirlpool tub, and it felt so nice she did not want to get out of it.

She heard his shower shut off, so she got out of the tub and dried off. By the time she had put her gown on, he was already in bed.

He said, "Peggy, I love you so much. Thanks for helping me make it possible for us to move back here. I never dreamed we would someday be living here.

I love the home that we had, but with Mom left here all alone after Dad died, I wanted to be close to care for her. I know dad would want this for her, also.

We know we cannot count on Terry to help us with Mom. He seldom called them, and visits were few and far apart.

I am not sure why he treats them like he has in the past, but I know they still loved him and wanted to share their home and land with me when they died. Mom did not have to let go of the house right now. She could have kept it until she died.

When she heard us say we wanted to be here closer, she decided to sell it to us. She knows she can count on you and me to be there for her. You became a daughter she never had, and she loves you so much. Peggy, you are so good to her and were to Dad when he was living.

I have always loved this farm and loved my mom and dad. We lived close but were not close enough to help them immediately in an emergency. Now, we will be here for her.

I am not sure how things will be for her with her health. She can still do lots of things for her age. I am glad we can be here together as a family.

This mattress is wonderful, and I love my shower. Peggy, you did a wonderful job picking out the things we needed for our bathroom and bedroom."

Peggy curled up in his arms and said, "I love you too, Tom. I am thrilled we were able to buy this house at this time.

I am looking forward to many years of joy and happiness here. I treasure the time we will have with Irene and love her like she was my mother.

My mother has been gone to be with the Lord, and I miss her, but I am thankful I have your mom I can love, and she loves me.

I love our new bedroom, which is downstairs close to hers. You and the other men in this family did a fabulous job of building this room so quickly.

I know Bobby and Eve will enjoy our home there and have a place they can call their own. Hopefully, the good Lord willing, they will know the joys of little ones to fill the house. I know they both want children. It is late, and I know you are very tired."

Leaning over, she kissed her husband goodnight, and in no time, he was fast asleep.

Lying there, she said a prayer of thanks to God for making it possible to be here. Having their place meant a lot to her. Charlie and Irene had taken loving care of this home. Now, it belonged to them.

In Rosewood, Bobby and Eve were spending their first night in the home they could call their home.

If she were right and the doctors were right, and she was pregnant, their children would enjoy this place and be in such a nice neighborhood. She was eager to go tomorrow and see if her suspicions were right about her being pregnant.

She was also grateful they were in a good school district.

Rolling over, she felt sleepy and drifted off to sleep.

After Davie and Jennifer got home, they told Marilyn how much they appreciated her taking care of the kids. She told them spending time with the grandkids was always enjoyable.

Davie took a shower after his mom left. When he got out of the shower, he was ready for bed.

He was glad they all worked hard and finished the work quickly. Now Tom and Peggy have moved into their house.

Davie was glad they were living here in Linkersville. He loved that they were close by so they could visit more often.

Jennifer was already in bed. She was not asleep and had turned back his covers for him. He slipped into bed next to her.

Jennifer said, "Davie, thanks for being here for me and the kids during this horrible, rough time from Rick raping me. I sure needed your love and support.

I had a terrible time re-adjusting to not only being raped but also losing the baby we both had looked forward to. I was also angry at what Rick did to me that caused me to miscarry our baby.

I am still harboring anger, and I know the upcoming trial here will be tough for you and me.

You have remarkable control of your feelings, and it took that control when Rick was found and arrested.

Rick had no right to take from me what he took. I love you so much, Davie, and I know I cannot show you how much currently, but my heart is full of love for you. Even a slight touch from someone is still hard. I hated Rick doing those things to me. His touching and raping me with such force and brutal acts was disgusting and horrible.

I fought him and tried my best to make him stop and not do that to me. As you know, there was no stopping him.

I am so glad he is behind bars now and will face the consequences of what he did to me and those other girls.

Hopefully, I can again enjoy being with you physically as we express our love. I miss those moments of happiness we share.

I love that we can still love each other in many other ways. For us, it is not all physical expressions.

I saw how considerate you have been as I have struggled to move beyond this horrible event in my life.

You have shown restraint and still showed me love and consideration. I knew I had your support and understanding."

Davie had listened to Jennifer as she opened up to him tonight and let her feelings be expressed.

He knew he needed to be there for her in other ways and was careful to be slow in reaching out to her. She was still fragile. He loved her so much and would do anything he could for her and help her start to heal.

He realized he might never be able to make love to her because of all the physical damage done to her. If they never made love to each other again, he would always show her love in every way he could and do so with such deep love and consideration.

Rick had torn her up inside, and he felt anger toward Rick for doing this to his beautiful wife. She did not deserve to be treated the way Rick had treated her.

Rick deserves the punishment that the courts will give him. He had no right to do this to her or those other innocent girls he exploited. With the help of the FBI and wonderful officers collaborating with him, he felt they had a strong rape case to present in court.

The young ladies taking the stand and telling their stories of how he raped them would strengthen the case.

The photos they found of Rick and some of those girls also prove his continual sexual abuse of young girls and women.

Jennifer could tell Davie was not asleep but in deep thought. She knew how much they both loved each other.

With love and prayers, she knew God would be there to help them both.

Davie turned towards her. Jenifer took his hand and held it in her hand. She moved close to him. He had such nice and caring hands. Holding his hand for a few moments, she turned his hand loose, and Davie gently wrapped his arm around her.

At first, she tensed up but let Davie gently hold her. She began to relax. His arms were gentle like the touch of his hand. It felt good to be held by the one she loved and who loved her.

Davie thanked God for those tender moments with Jennifer. It meant so much to him that she could allow him near her and reach out to him.

He was so blessed to have her in his life. He had loved her from the moment he first saw her at her grandparents, standing in the snow in a white snowsuit, looking like an angel to him.

Jennifer had drifted off to sleep. He carefully and gently removed his arm from around her so he would not startle her or wake her.

The next morning, Davie woke up to the aroma of coffee. Jennifer was up and had made them coffee.

When Jennifer entered their bedroom with two cups of coffee, Davie sat up in bed. Davie reached for the two cups so that she could crawl back in bed with him.

Jennifer got in bed and sat up with her pillow behind her back. Davie handed her one of the cups of coffee. Neither one spoke, but he could not help but look at her as he sipped his coffee.

Jennifer sat her cup of coffee on the nightstand and said, "Glad you woke up. We have the entire world out there waiting for us. I am so glad we can continue our journey in life together. I love you, Davie."

Davie sat his coffee cup down, and about that time, two little kids came running into their room and crawled up in bed with them.

Jenny was chattering up a storm and telling her mother about their fun with Grandma Marilyn.

Jimmy was over by his dad, just laughing. He said, "Dad, can we go fishing sometime soon?"

Davie said, "We sure can. You need to check out our fishing lures, son, and see if we need to buy any more fishing gear."

Hugging his son, he told him they must prepare for church after breakfast.

They would be going every Sunday. They could check out their fishing gear after church and might go sit down by the lake and see if they can catch any fish after they get home.

The sermon their pastor preached was great. It was like God had given him a sermon they needed.

In his sermon, the scriptures spoke of forgiveness, controlling our anger, and praying for those who spitefully hurt us.

It spoke of turning to God. We should leave our heartaches and problems in his hands and look to Him for strength and courage through prayers and acts of faith.

In these actions of faith, we can find healing for our hearts, mind, body, and soul.

Davie and Jimmy went fishing when they got home.

Jennifer and Jenny drove to where her mom and dad lived now, in grandma's house, which now is their house, including Grandma Irene.

Jenny loved doing things with her mom. She did not understand why her mama was not feeling good sometimes, but she loved her and was glad it was okay for them to hug her and sit on her lap.

Arriving at her mom and dad's place, they greeted them on the porch. Grandma was also with them.

What a beautiful picture of the three of them. It made her sad; Grandpa was not there, but he was with God, and she would see him again.

Everyone hugged Jenny and asked her if she had come to help them. She said, "Yes, I am a good helper. I keep my dishes on the shelf in my room and am incredibly careful with my dishes."

They hugged her again and said, "Well, we are glad you and your mom are here to help us."

Grandma Irene gave Jenny some things she could put on the shelf in the pantry. She was careful and loved getting to help.

With everyone working, moving, and changing things around, they had unpacked, and the kitchen looked great.

Grandma Irene's pots, pans, and dishes were still in the cabinet. Charlie had built many cabinets, so there was plenty of space for Peggy's things and Grandma Irene's dishes.

Most large pots and pans not used daily were on shelves in the pantry and were easy to reach. Some electrical appliances were in the pantry.

Peggy and Irene stood there admiring their work, and both agreed they would enjoy all those dishes, pots, and pans. The kitchen looked great.

There would be a lot of family gatherings here, and those dishes and other things would be needed.

After Davie and Jimmy decided the fish were not biting today, they put away their fishing gear. They drove to Tom and Peggy's place to see them and Grandma Irene.

Tom was out in the tool shop. He had been moving and rearranging things to make room for the tools he had brought when he moved here. Davie and Jimmy pitched in and helped him.

Jimmy was fascinated with the tools. He wanted to learn how to use them. Tom and Davie told him they would work in this tool shop and teach him how to use some tools. He would learn about some of the other tools when he got older.

Davie said, "Charlie would be thrilled knowing his oldest son lives here now and cares for his sweetheart."

Tom said, "I had been here to visit the weekend before he passed away. I asked him how he felt about Peggy and me moving back here. He was thrilled.

Dad had told me, "Son, I am so glad to know you will be close by and look out for my precious wife.

I love my son Terry, but he has other interests in life, and moving here was not something he would ever do.

I am unsure what kind of home you are looking for, son, but Irene cannot care for a place this big by herself.

Glad you are coming home. You and Terry will inherit this place when I am gone. She can remain here for as long as God permits, or her health will permit.

She can also sell it herself but must give you the first chance to buy it. I know you will make sure Terry gets his part of the money.

I love both of you and when I am gone, it makes me feel good to know you will be here for your mom."

Tom said, "My dad took care of this place. I marvel at how he kept it so nice when he got older. Look at this garage. Everything and every tool has a special place.

Lots of good memories here with him in this tool shop. He taught me also to put the tools back where I found them."

CHAPTER 9

The End

The day of the trial had been changed several times. Rick's mother had tried every way she could to get Rick out of jail and delay the court date.

The lawyer she found for Rick had to keep reminding her of the laws and what they could and could not do legally. It wasn't easy working with her on behalf of her son. She made his job a lot harder.

The previous trial date set for Rick several years ago, when he appeared before the court for attempted rape charges, made it harder this time for him with these rape charges against him after he was a no-show for the court hearing of the charges of attempted rape.

His failure to appear for the previous charges and leaving the country would not be good with this Judge.

The lawyer said he would do his best to represent Rick Goldman as best he could regarding this rape charge and the loss of her baby due to the rape.

The plaintiff had plenty of medical evidence to support her story, and her baby's death would also be judged today. His client was not extremely helpful in preparing the case. Rick was angry because he did not get him out of jail.

He was angry with his mother because she was not successful in paying whatever it took to get him out of jail.

Rick's lawyer could not locate anyone who would testify in court about his good behavior and what a nice person he was. Most people told Rick was spoiled and got everything he wanted, thanks to his wealthy mother.

No one ever said "Yes" to him about testifying about him being a nice person.

After several delays requested by the lawyer, the Judge told him no more delays and set the date for the hearing. That date had arrived.

The pastor from Davie and Jennifer's church was there in the courtroom. When they arrived, he told Jennifer and her family that the church had met today and had a circle of prayers to God on their behalf. They also sent their love and support to each one.

Everyone was seated and ready for the trial to begin. The Judge entered the room. Everyone stood up until the Judge sat down behind his desk. Striking the gavel, he let everyone know they were ready for this trial to begin. Everyone sat down, and the trial began.

The Judge gave instructions regarding the proceedings and reminded each attorney of the case and how the proceedings would be conducted.

The Judge read Plaintiff Jennifer Vaughn; charges of brutal rape, loss of her unborn baby due to the brutality of the rape, and brutal force, which caused her baby's life and almost cost her life.

The Judge gave Jennifer's lawyer a chance to submit these claims of rape, and he would prove, beyond any doubt, that Rick Goldman viciously raped Ms. Vaughn.

Rick Goldman intentionally and deliberately did this rape without her consent for sex.

Rick Goldman's lawyer presented his case briefly.

The lawyer knew all he could do was make sure Rick had legal representation and all laws were being met thru the process.

The Judge said the Plaintiff could go first. He told Jennifer she would approach the bench, be sworn in, and sit on the witness stand.

The Judge told Mr. Goldman's lawyer he would get his chance to tell his side of the story when the lawyer for Ms. Vaughn had finished presenting their case.

The lawyer for Ms. Vaughn stood up and told the Judge they had several witnesses that had agreed to take the stand regarding Jennifer being raped by Rick Goldman and their own rape experiences of being forcibly raped by Rick Goldman.

Copies of all three witnesses had been made available to the Judge concerning their written testimony regarding being raped by Rick Goldman.

The Judge told Mr. Goldman's attorney all the witnesses would be heard first, and then his client's story could be presented.

Jennifer had dreaded this day. As she testified, the love and support of her family and God's presence in her life would help her.

Being on the witness stand gave her a chance to tell her story of how she was raped.

She also hoped that going first would be helpful to two young girls when they testified.

Jennifer started her testimony by sharing Rick's attempt to rape her when he had dated her while she was still in High School.

Despite his flowers, jewelry, and eating in all the best places, she began to see a pattern of behavior that troubled her. He would get angry with her if he made advances and gestures of wanting her to have sex when she pushed him away and said, "No."

She told him the night she broke up with him, the reason it was over between them. She was tired of saying "No" and pushing him away. Each time they dated, he was more aggressive, and she felt it best for them to stop dating.

He became incredibly angry and told her, "Jennifer, you have told me "No" your last time. No one says No to me and gets away with it.

This will be my last date with you, but I will get what I want from you tonight. "

He began tearing at my blouse while holding my wrist. One hand was free to reach behind me for the door handle. Finding the door handle, I opened the door and leaned toward the opening. I fell out of his grip and out of his car.

I jumped up and tried to run, but he caught me and threw me to the ground.

I resisted him in every way I could. He was tearing at my clothes when a stranger saw what was happening as he drove up. He jumped out of his vehicle and dragged Rick off me. The stranger hit him and knocked him out cold.

When he saw my blouse was ripped off me, He took his shirt off and put it on me. Then he took me back up to Rick's car. He told me to get inside the car and lock the doors.

He said," I will call the police officers, and they will come and help you. Then he got into his car and left."

A female police officer was with the other officers when the police arrived. She was so kind and caring. She brought a blanket and put it around me.

She told me they would take me to the hospital so I could get medical care and tests could be done.

I was shaking when I arrived at the hospital. They did the necessary test and examinations for a rape victim. They charted all evidence in me and my clothing and a full report regarding him trying to rape me.

They called my mom and dad. My mom and dad came to the hospital and was there for me during all the test and examinations.

I was so glad to have my mother and dad there. She had brought me some clothes I could put on later.

It was a tough time for me. Rick would have raped me that night if the stranger had not shown up in time to rescue me.

I never did anything to encourage him. I wanted to wait to have sex until I got married. I wanted to have sex for the first time with my husband on our wedding night. I was really upset.

It took me months of therapy to move on with my life. The night I got home from him almost raping me, I felt dirty from him trying to do this to me and disgusted because he had forcibly tried to rape me."

Jennifer sat silent for a few minutes. Tears came to her eyes as she remembered.

The Judge said, "Would you like to take a break for a few minutes." Jennifer nodded yes.

The judge said, "We will take a 15-minute recess."

After we return, Ms. Vaughn, you will be asked to return to the witness stand and be reminded you are still under oath. You may step down and join your family. As she left the stand, she heard Rick say, "Jennifer."

Before Rick could say another word, the Judge told him, "Rick Goldman, you are to sit down, be quiet, and stay seated until Plaintiff and her family are escorted from the courtroom."

The Judge nodded to Davie and said, "Mr. Vaughn, come forward and escort your wife from the courtroom."

One of the court officers escorted the family to a room where they could be alone.

Hugging Jennifer, they each reassured her that she had their prayers, love, and full support. They knew this would be very painful, bringing up the experience of Rick's attempt to rape her.

Jennifer knew this was something she had to do since Rick had raped her when he returned from Europe, where he had been hiding from the law.

While they waited, Jennifer said, "Davie, as I spoke of losing our baby girl because he had raped me, I realized we had never given our baby a name.

Do you like the name Janie Irene for the baby we lost? I chose that name because that is my grandma Irene's middle name.

The first name Jane would give us three children whose first name starts with a J. We would have our twins, Jimmy Joe and Jenny Sue, my middle name, and then our baby girl, Janie Irene."

He told her it was a perfect name for their baby girl.

A rap on the door meant it was time to return to the courtroom. The officer was there to escort them back to the courtroom.

The Judge entered the room, and everyone stood until the Judge was behind his desk. Rapping the Gavel on his desk, he told everyone to sit down, and they would resume the court hearing.

After being reminded she was still under oath, she was asked to return to the witness stand.

Sitting in the chair, she reminded herself to focus on God and let the words come out pleasing to God, who was with her that day on the stand.

The scripture her grandmother reminded her of was John 14:27: "Peace I leave with you, my peace I give unto you; not as the world giveth, give I unto you. Let not your heart be troubled, neither let it be afraid."

The Judge told her she could resume her testimony.

Jennifer said, "What I am about to share with you is very painful for me to share.

It is necessary to let you know what happened to me recently and why I had to file charges against Rick Goldman.

My husband was out of town doing investigative work for the police department. I knew he would be returning that morning.

I dressed and decided to change the sheets and wash and hang them on the line. After this, I sat on our porch with a cup of coffee. The breeze and warm sun felt so nice as I sat there sipping my coffee.

I heard a car coming down our long driveway to our house. I thought it might be my husband getting home earlier than he had told me on the phone. Rising from my chair, I saw a red Corvette in front of the house. I knew this was not my husband's car.

I wondered if someone was lost and needed directions to locate a certain place. I did not recognize this car.

When the driver exited the car and came up on the porch, he had blonde hair. He was wearing sunglasses, and I never realized it was Rick Goldman until he took off his sunglasses, and I saw those eyes and knew it was him.

I realized by that look on his face that he had come out of hiding to keep the promise he had screamed at me when he left the courtroom.

Previously, he was supposed to have been in court, and the Judge had given him a date to return for the hearing, but instead had fled to another country while he was out on bail.

His mom had him out of jail by paying an enormous bail bond amount. He never appeared in court on that date, and the police had no luck finding him to serve him with a warrant for his arrest for failing to appear in court.

He was handcuffed when he left the courthouse at that first appearance for the attempted rape charges. He screamed out to me that promise he said to me, "Jennifer, I will be back and will get what I want. No one ever says "No" to me. I always get what I want."

I knew from what he had previously said that day that he had returned and was now standing on my porch. I tried to get inside the house to lock the door, but he was too fast for me.

My phone was in the kitchen, and he had a death grip on me as he dragged me across the floor.

I was screaming, trying to get loose, and begging him not to do this. He dragged me to what was our bedroom. He threw me on the bed, holding my wrists in his hand.

I screamed and pleaded with him not to do what I knew he would do. He slapped me hard and told me to shut up as he proceeded to get what he came for. I resisted him in every way I could, but he was too strong for me.

I told him I was pregnant and please not do what he was doing and stop. He hit me so hard that time, and it knocked me unconscious.

When I came to, he was gone. I was in horrible pain. I knew I was bleeding and needed to get help so I would not lose my baby. I dragged myself across the floor to get to my phone. I lost consciousness again.

Davie had tried to call me when he was getting closer to home. When I did not answer after several attempts to reach me, he knew something was wrong.

He called the police department and told them that he would be back in town soon and asked them if they had an officer working in the area where he lived. They told him they had an officer less than a ½ mile from his house.

The police records show what is in their report and what they found when they entered our house.

A cup of coffee was sitting on the table on the porch. Clothes were hung on the clotheslines.

The front door was open when the police arrived and called my name. No one had answered. He called for some backups because the door was wide open, and not even the screen door was locked. I learned from the police report that another officer arrived and entered the house.

As they entered to their left near the end of the island, they found me lying on the floor and unconscious. Some blood was on the floor, and the officer saw bruises on my face and arms. They called for an ambulance.

They called Davie, letting him know what they found at his house and that they had called an ambulance when they saw blood on the floor."

Jennifer paused for a few minutes from testifying. This was harder than she could imagine, having to be on a witness stand and reliving the horrors of what happened, with the rapist sitting only a few feet from her.

Jennifer continued with her testimony. After a few sips of water, she allowed God's presence to overflow.

Continuing her testimony, she said, "I had always been fearful Rick would come back but had hoped he never would return."

I arrived at the hospital unconscious after being raped. The examination at the hospital revealed I had been raped and needed to go to surgery to try and save my baby.

They told me later that the trauma and brutal force of his rape had caused my baby to be born prematurely.

The doctor had done a C-section to save our baby while she was still alive, but my baby died.

With tears streaming down Jennifer's face, she continued to tell the horrible story of how he raped her.

The Judge decided to take another break. He knew the witness needed some more time to regain her composure.

Striking his gavel, he said, "Time for a recess."

The Judge told Jennifer she could return to her husband and family.

A police officer made sure everyone stayed seated until the plaintiff and family were in the room they used before. Davie held her hand as they returned to the room. She regained her composure and had time with family and God.

After a 15-minute break, Jennifer and her family returned to the courtroom.

The Judge told Jennifer to return to the witness stand, and she was still under oath.

Jennifer said, "Thank you, Judge, for the recess. "I am ready to complete my testimony."

"During my stay in the hospital, it was several weeks before I woke up from being unconscious.

The doctor entered my room, and I asked him, " How is my baby? I was afraid I had lost my baby because I could no longer feel the baby when I ran my hand across my stomach. I only felt stitches where they had done the C Section.

The doctor said, "Jennifer, I am so sorry to tell you that we could not save your baby. We did our best to save her by doing the C-section, but the trauma to your baby was too much, and she died in surgery."

Jennifer said, "I thanked the doctor for his efforts to save the baby, and then turned to Davie and told him how sorry I was we had lost our baby girl because of the rape."

I went into a deep state of unconsciousness after hearing my baby died because of Rick raping me."

"Jennifer started sobbing as she realized again why she lost her baby."

Most of the ones in the courtroom had tears in their eyes as they listened to her story and heard the horrible way she was raped, a rape that caused her to lose her baby.

Drying her tears, Jennifer continued, saying, "After this happened to me, I woke up from unconsciousness and would not let anyone touch me. The nurses and doctors understood and cared for me however they could.

When I left the hospital, arrived home, and started upon my porch, I turned and walked down the driveway, trying to escape from the memories of Rick dragging me from the porch and taking me inside the house to the bedroom that was mine and Davie's.

I have had therapy, a loving family, God's presence, great doctors, and wonderful support to help me recover from this rape.

I will live with the memories of this for the rest of my life, but I refuse to let them destroy me.

When I got home from the hospital, I also saw the pain in my two children's eyes when they ran to me and hugged me. I screamed from pain and pushed them away because of the physical and emotional pain from the rape.

I knew when I looked into their eyes I had to find a way to survive and be able to allow my family, my husband, and my children to be able to touch me and for me to be able to reach out to them.

Rick took from me what was not his to take. He almost cost me my life and caused me to lose my baby and my ability to reach out to my husband, children, and family again.

I made up my mind with therapy and their help to learn how to cope with those horrible things he had done to me and move on with my life.

Rick can no longer hurt me or any of these girls he raped.

We are here today, as painful as it has been to tell my story, and it will be for them to let you know how Rick Goldman has treated us and taken advantage of us against our will.

I have testified to you the events and did so truthfully, and the evidence supports these claims of rape." Jennifer turned to the Judge.

She said, "Thank you, your honor, for your kindness, patience, and for allowing me breaks so I could share with you what happened the day Rick Goldman returned to get what he promised he would get because he had told me.

"I will be back, and I will get what I came back for, and no one ever tells me "No" because I always get what I want."

The Judge nodded to Davie to come forward. When he did, he turned to Davie and said, "I am glad she has you and this family to turn to for love and support. You may escort your wife to a seat beside you."

The Judge said, "We have two more witnesses from two young ladies who will tell their stories of how Rick Goldman raped them when they were still in High School.

There is also evidence in this folder here, which I am holding up, to support these claims of rape.

Since it is lunchtime, we will take a break, have lunch, and meet back here at 2:00 p.m."

Striking the gavel, he dismissed Jennifer and her family. Then, after they left the courtroom, he dismissed the remaining ones in the court.

The officers took Rick back to jail to be held until it was time to return to court.

Davie, Jennifer, and her family found a wonderful place to eat where they could eat, sit, and talk in privacy. Jennifer was quiet during their meal.

Davie was watching Jennifer. She was in a daze as she sat there eating her food. Jennifer sat quietly praying for those two young ladies who would be testifying when they returned to the courthouse. She knew how hard it had been for her to tell her story of how she was raped and who raped her.

Jennifer also knew the testimonies of these two young ladies would make her case even stronger for the kind of man Rick was.

They, too, had resisted him, but he raped them anyway. They also had evidence to support their claims of rape.

When they returned to the courthouse, the Judge was in the room, and everyone was seated; the court was ready to start the next proceedings.

The Judge called the first young lady to the stand after she was sworn in.

She said, "When I learned about Jennifer being raped by Rick, I knew I needed to find the courage to testify in court what Rick Goldman had done to me.

He had also raped me several years ago when I was still a student in High School. What he did to me was cruel, and I did not give him consent and tried to stop him, but he was too strong for me. He told me the same thing he told Jennifer: he always got what he wanted.

Had I known that the flowers and gifts were given to me because he thought lavishing me with gifts, nice places to eat, flowers, and other things were for him to get what he deserved and wanted sex, I would have never dated him. begged him not to rape me, and he raped me anyway. He did not have my consent to have sex with him.

I am here today to testify that I also had to have therapy and lots of help. I told my parents that night when I got home what he had done to me.

They took me to the hospital, and tests and exams were done. I was devastated and felt so dirty and molested by what he did to me during the rape.

My parents wanted me to report the rape and take him to court, but I was too scared. I was afraid of what else he might do to me if I had him arrested.

I did not want anyone to know this had happened to me because it was so awful. I did not even tell my friends what he had done to me.

I am glad I had a good relationship with my parents and could talk to them and let them know.

The therapist I saw was wonderful. She helped me be able to put this behind me.

I knew today I would bring it all back and relive that rape. Still, I felt with all Jennifer had gone through and survived and was able to testify today, that I needed to find the courage to do the same thing today and testify; looking straight at Rick, she turned toward him and said, "Rick you got what you wanted back then, but now we are here to tell our stories, of how you raped us."

She looked back at the Judge and said, "That is my testimony for today."

After leaving the witness box, she returned to her seat. The next witness was called into the courtroom. She was sworn in and took her seat on the witness stand.

Turning to the Judge, she said, "I am ready to tell my story of how Rick Goldman raped me."

Turning back to those in the room, she momentarily turned toward Rick and looked at him. Suddenly all the events of the night he raped her were so visible. She had successfully pushed those horrible moments away all these years since the rape.

Looking back toward Jennifer, she saw the courage Jennifer had today and the pain in her eyes and voice as she talked about the events surrounding how Rick raped her. Dropping her head, she also saw the pain of a mother who had lost her baby.

"Judge and to each of you, I am here today to tell of this horrible experience that occurred in my life because I was raped.

As I sat and listened to Jennifer and Katie tell you about their experiences, I almost lost my courage to witness today.

I realize, though, that by being silent, I am allowing Rick to get away with this, once again, and by force, always got what he wanted, and that was sex, even against our will or consent.

Rick would love it if none of us took the stand today. I knew, though, that he had hurt me and these two who have also testified.

None of us deserved to be raped. We were nice girls, believed in God, and wanted to keep ourselves pure so that someday, when the right person came into our lives, we could go to him on our wedding night, pure and undefiled.

Therapy helped me, and my parents also helped me realize I was not impure or unworthy of life with that special person I married.

It was not my fault that he took something from me that was not his to take. I resisted, pushed, screamed, and did everything possible to keep him from raping me. I also begged him not to rape me."

Rick only laughed and said, "Girl, you owed me this. I have done a lot to show you an enjoyable time, and I think you should consider this dessert for the evening."

I struggled and tried to escape him, but he overpowered me with his strength and raped me, and tore me up inside from being so rough and brutal.

Later, when he dropped me off at the house, I barely walked to the door. I was a virgin, and he was cruel.

My mom heard the car leave and went to the door. I was sitting on a step, crying, and holding myself. My dad came to the door, and they wrapped their arms around me. I was unable even to tell them what was wrong with me.

They took me to the hospital when Dad saw I needed medical care. They did those tests and exams that Jennifer and Katie got at the hospital.

They kept me overnight because I was torn and bleeding. I should have taken the advice of the rape counselor at the hospital and reported Rick, but I was scared and hurting.

The doctor told me before I left the hospital that he was concerned about my physical condition and hoped the damage done to me would not prevent me from being able to have children. The doctor was hopeful that I would heal and recover okay.

Years of therapy helped me put this behind me. When I learned about what Rick did to Jennifer, I was horrified to think he had done this to someone else.

I wished I had dared to have reported him as the one who had raped me. If I had reported him, these two other witnesses would not have had to go through what they went through.

Years have passed, and I remain single. I might not ever have children because of the damage done internally to me when I was raped and was so young when that happened.

Thank you for listening and giving us this opportunity to speak today. Thanks to time, healing, and therapy, I could come today.

I know justice will be served in this courtroom, but it will not erase what we have gone through by Rick raping us.

Jennifer and Katie, God is still with us, and we can now face tomorrow with those we love. God is there to provide for us what we need to live with what was done to us. The future is there for us now to look to the future without fear of Rick returning anymore to take revenge on us."

Turning to the Judge, she said, "That is my testimony today."

The Judge told her she could return to her seat.

Picking up some photos in one hand and folders in the other hand, the Judge said, the evidence is also right here in my hands of Rick Goldman's rapes.

I have studied and read all the reports contained in these files. I have examined all the evidence and the ages of the girls when they were raped.

I have seen photos of him with these witnesses, and it is obvious from some of those photos they were unconscious, and their clothes had been ripped from them.

There are also some depositions from several girls still in Jr. High School whom Rick had raped. These young ladies could not come today but have those depositions of their accounts of rape in these files. Some of these girls were underage.

All the evidence shows a pattern of behavior over the years by Rick Goldman regarding sex.

I have read all the material presented to me by the police department of evidence of rape by Rick Goldman.

The stories today are truthful and match the evidence I hold. We are here to bring justice and enforce laws when someone violates the laws."

Rick's mother stood up and said, "I have heard enough today. My son is good, and he does not deserve to be dragged through this court with these accusations of rape.

These girls encouraged him, and he gave them what they wanted. Oh yes, they scream rape now, but he only gave them what he thought they wanted.

Jennifer's baby died because it was not a healthy baby. My son is not responsible for the loss of her child."

The judge said, "Ms. Goldman, you are out of order and need to remain seated in your chair and quiet.

You are part of the reason your son behaves the way he does. You encouraged him to get whatever he wanted regardless of the cost. By what you say, you are only making things worse for your son today."

The judge returned to everyone and said, "Ms. Goldman did everything she could to stop these proceedings today.

When her son was in court for his attempted rape, she paid the extremely high bail money and got him out of jail.

She also took him out of the country so he would not have to appear in court. Laws were violated when she did that.

Today we are looking at brutal, forceful rape without consent, leaving the country before a hearing for his attempted rape charges, raping several minors, and physically hitting, slapping, and preventing those he raped from being able to stop him.

Some other charges will also be a part of my decision today. His mother's attempt to bribe the police and me as Judge of this hearing will also be dealt with today."

Turning to the lawyers representing their clients, the Judge asked if they had other witnesses or evidence that had not been presented.

Did they have anything they wished to say in this courtroom today concerning their clients that had not been presented?

Both lawyers told the Judge they had nothing more to say or add to what had been said. They rested their cases.

The judge returned to Rick and said, "Mr. Rick Goldman, the court wishes you to stand up and face me.

I have all this evidence of your raping several young ladies against their wishes and without their consent.

I have reviewed the evidence, and that alone speaks of your guilt, without even the testimonies of these young ladies today.

Rick Goldman, you are guilty on all counts of rape and rape of minors.

You skipped the country before your hearing for the attempted rape charges, so leaving the country with sufficient evidence regarding your attempt and returning to rape Jennifer is also a part of my decisions.

The evidence those other two witnesses submitted also points to your quilt of rape.

The loss of life of Jennifer's baby is also a crime. You molested, brutally raped, and hit her, knocking her unconscious. The medical reports show the baby was alive when Jennifer was raped. The baby died from the trauma you forced on Jennifer when you raped her while she was pregnant.

This carries many years in prison for this rape alone and the loss of her baby. Jennifer was forced, and Katie, our last witness, to live with the fear of your retaliation if they reported you to the Police.

Rick Goldman, you need help. You have had a pattern of abuse of girls and women.

You used your money to impress them and make them like you, but you only wanted one thing to get what you wanted from them, and that was sex.

Today, you are sentenced to 30 years in prison without parole."

"Officers, will you take Mr. Rick Goldman back to jail? I want heavy security and guards to ensure he does not leave that jail. I have spoken to the prison, and they are prepared to pick him up today at the jail and take him to prison.

Everyone else in court remains seated. When the Officer calls and tells me he is securely locked in jail, you will be free to leave the courthouse.

As six officers and others outside escorted Rick out of the courtroom, you could hear him screaming, kicking, swearing, and hollering at his mother, "You told me you had enough money to get me out of this."

The Judge stood up and said to the officers, "Bring him back into this courtroom." They took him back.

The Judge told Rick Goldman, "No amount of money will get you out of raping these girls and women, and I do not allow the profanity I heard in my courtroom. You will leave quietly because I will have them gag you if you do not. You are guilty and will leave here not kicking and screaming."

The Judge then turned to Rick's parents and told them, "You are not free to leave this courtroom yet.   I have a few things to say to you."

Turning to Ms. Goldman, the Judge said, "I know you thought letting him have everything he wanted was okay. You created the son, who left for jail because he learned you would pay out money to get him out of jail or pay off the Judge or officers for a lighter sentence.

If you attempt any more capers as you did in the past to get him out of jail and out of the country, you will be standing here before me.

I will make sure you pay for your attempts to free him again. Goldman family, you can leave the courthouse now."

The judge turned to Jennifer and her family and the two witnesses and their families as victims.

"He said, "It is so sad, and I am so sorry you have all had to experience these traumas in your life. Nothing I do or say today will erase those things from your memory.

Move on with your lives, knowing the one who raped you has been sent to prison for many years. Now, you can live in peace without fearing his returning to harm you again.

Sitting in this courtroom with the one who raped you took courage. You did the right thing today with your testimonies, so we could put Rick Goldman behind bars so he cannot rape or hurt any other young girls or women.

You are all special young ladies, and I want you to move on with your lives, put these memories away again, and enjoy life again.

Recovery takes time. Reliving this trauma has stirred those memories, but today, walk out of here determined to allow God, your families, and loved ones to help you live a full and wonderful life. You are worthy of being loved by those who love you.

The witnesses and evidence helped make it possible for me to send him to prison for 30 years with no parole.

To each family here today, of these young ladies, thank you for your love and support of your beautiful, special young daughters.

You will be escorted to your cars today. All precautions will be taken to ensure your safety until he is in prison.

The Police Chief has just sent word that he is behind bars, so you can leave here without fear of his escaping from being taken to jail."

Rapping his gavel, he said, "Court is adjourned, and case closed."

Chief Taylor called Davie when they had Rick behind bars in jail.

He told Davie, "When the officers had brought Rick from the court, he had been very combative and hard to manage. They had enough officers to hold him and get him behind bars in jail. They put him in a jail cell that was padded.

Within one hour, the correctional officers were here at the police station. I told the corrections officers how combative he was and difficult to manage when they brought him from the courthouse.

One of the guards went out to their vehicle and got a straitjacket. Four officers went into Rick's cell to help hold him while they put him in a straitjacket.

After they finally got him ready to leave, he started cussing and screaming at them. One of the correctional officers put a gag on him, and Rick was furious.

Once they left the station with Rick, several police officers followed them to the prison.

As you know, Davie, the prison is not too far from Rosewood. I am glad we can close that case now."

After Rick's mom and dad left the courthouse, Rick's mom was already trying to find a way to get her son out of prison and get the verdict overturned.

She had not been happy with the lawyer they had. She had paid him good money to do the needed job to keep Rick out of prison.

The lawyer refused to do what she wanted to be done, knowing those actions were illegal. She was furious.

On the way back to their house from the courthouse, Mr. Goldman turned to his wife and said, "I know you thought spoiling him and getting him out of scrapes he got into was the right thing to do for our son.

Even now, after the Judge warned you about some of your actions, you still want to do illegal and wrong things.

If you do one more thing to try to get our son out of prison, which is illegal, I will report you to the Judge. Not only will I report you, but I will also leave you. Your money is not enough to keep me in this marriage.

I was ashamed of our son and what he had become. Hearing those young ladies testify how he treated and raped them was horrible.

What he did was wrong, and he put those young women through some horrible things because he likes getting what he wants and will not take "No" for an answer. I love our son, but you have helped make it possible for him to become the kind of man he is today.

I have tried to get you to see this over the years, but you were determined that your son would have everything money could buy.

You wanted him to do whatever he wanted to do that he liked doing. You bought him anything he wanted."

She never spoke a word while her husband was talking. He had never fully understood their son and his needs.

When she got home, she called the airport and told them to get her jet ready; she would fly out that day. She gave them the place she was flying to, hung up the phone, and packed her bags.

The limo was waiting outside for her. She stopped at the door, turned to her husband, and said, "You will hear from my attorney. It is over between us. I do not need you in my life anymore. You will get a settlement from me and the divorce papers."

The following week, the papers and a check arrived from her lawyer. He put the money into a new bank account. He told the housekeeper he was leaving, and she would get instructions regarding the house there in Rosewood.

She was a beautiful, sweet, and lovable woman when he married her. She inherited her father's estate after he passed away. The money and her love of it destroyed her.

Their marriage had been over for a long time. He never liked divorces. He did his best to stay in the marriage because he loved her.

Over the years, his love for her had changed because of the kind of person she became after Rick was born.

He still loved the woman he married, but the one who walked out of the house and sent him the divorce papers was not the one he had fallen in love with many years ago.

The Warden at the prison called Chief Taylor and let him know the prisoner was in his cell. He thanked the police department for the assistance and the officers following them to the prison.

The Warden said, "This prisoner has much to learn about prison life. It is not all about him getting his way about everything."

Chief Taylor called Davie. He said, "Davie, thanks for all the work you did to get the information regarding Rick Goldman. Rick is behind bars in prison.

I have closed the file on Rick Goldman. I will call the other families and thank them for their cooperation and the ones who were witnesses. It was a compelling case against the rapist, and the Judge gave him the maximum prison sentence.

Give Jennifer our love and tell her we were behind her all the way, and so glad she could find the strength to tell the whole story with Rick sitting in the courtroom.

Davie, with this case closed, how about you take a few days off to spend with the family? I will call you if something requires you to come to the office."

Davie thanked the Chief and hung up the phone.

Turning to Jennifer, he said, "Rick is imprisoned behind bars. My boss said he thought I should take some time off from work and spend some time with family."

Jennifer said, "I want us to go on a trip. I think the kids would love doing some things with us that are fun for them.

I am exhausted from court today but would enjoy getting away for a few days."

Davie said, "Sweetheart, you figure out some things we can all do, and if you need help making plans, call me, and I will help you with the plans. I must call my mom and dad and tell them Rick is behind bars in a prison cell."

CHAPTER 10

"Mom, that Bear Scared Me!"

Jennifer called her mom and dad. Her mother answered the phone.

Jennifer said, "Good morning, Mom. I called to inform you that Davie has been given several days off from work. He thought Davie deserved some time off with his family.

We talked about things to do together as a family. Mom, can you share any suggestions with us regarding places and things to do?

Peggy said, "Well, when you were kids about that age, you always had fun camping out.

We still have that pop-up trailer we used when we went camping. Your dad moved it up here to the farm. It is in one of the sheds."

Jennifer said, "Okay, Mom, but I do not recall some places where we went camping. I do remember the fun we had together. Bobby and I enjoyed camping."

Peggy said, "Some nice state parks are not too far from us. We camped at one of those parks but did not recall which one."

Jennifer said, "Okay, Davie just came home, so I will run that possibility by him and see what he thinks. Talk to you later. Thanks, Mom, Bye."

He thought it was a great idea when Jennifer told him about talking with her mom and suggesting camping and using their camper.

Davie and Jennifer drove to visit her mom and dad, and Davie wanted to check out the camper.

When they arrived, Tom took Davie down to the shed, and they pushed the trailer out.

It was a nice camper, and everything inside was in decent shape when they popped the top up. They checked the refrigerator and other things they would use and be ready for camping.

The kids were so excited when they heard they were all going camping. Jimmy was thrilled because he knew he would spend much time with his mom and dad.

He asked his grandpa if they were going camping, too. His grandpa Tom said, "Not this time. We might go later this summer. This camping trip is for just the four of you."

Grandma Irene found their picnic basket and a few other things nice to have when you are camping. She knew they could use those things and brought them to Jennifer.

Jennifer had not even thought about what they needed to take when camping.

She was grateful her grandmother knew what was needed when you go camping, and she took the things and put them in the camper.

Tom hooked up the trailer to Davie's truck, and they pulled it home. Davie loved the trailer. It pulled nice behind the truck.

They would enjoy camping in it. Much nicer than a tent, which Davie had used in the past when he went camping.

Jennifer and her mother had written down things to take with her for meals and other items. When she got home, she started checking off the list and getting the things together to take with them.

Davie loaded everything needed in the camper, and before he dropped the top back down, the kids had come out there where he was loading the camper.

They both climbed inside and decided who slept in which bunk. Jimmy wanted the top bunk.

He left the bottom bunk for Jenny because he did not think it wise to have Jenny sleep up on the top bunk and climb the ladder to get in or out of bed. He did not want her to fall from that top bunk. A nice double bed was on one end of the trailer for his mom and dad. It had a porta-pot for them to use. The kitchen was nice. There was a small refrigerator and stove for cooking. The sink was small.

Davie finished what he was doing, and everyone got out of the camper after he had secured everything for traveling. He was ready to drop the top-down, lock it in place, and it was ready for them to go camping.

Davie had found several parks near them. They chose the one that had a fishing area and swimming area.

They loaded into the truck the next morning and headed to the state park. When they arrived, it sure looked like the perfect place to camp.

The park ranger met them at the camp and directed them to the area they had reserved for their camper. Davie set up the camper and popped up the top of the camper. He ensured everything was okay inside, and Jennifer took some things from the truck and put them in the camper.

Davie set up lawn chairs for them outside the camper. Jennifer and Jenny sat down in their lawn chairs. Jenny and Jimmy both had kid-size fold-up lawn chairs.

Jimmy and his dad decided to go fishing. They got the fishing gear out of the truck and took off to the lake just below where they were camping. Jennifer and Jenny sat in their lawn chairs and watched Davie and Jimmy at the lake fishing. Jimmy had caught a fish and was excited. Davie helped him get it off his hook. They were having an enjoyable time.

Jenny said, "Mom, I hear the birds singing. A little squirrel ran up that tree and is looking at me," she giggled.

Jennifer closed her eyes and listened to the birds singing. It was so peaceful, quiet, and a good place to camp.

Jenny looked over at her mom and screamed. "Mama, AH - AH—there is a big black bear behind you."

Davie and Jimmy heard the scream and ran up to the trailer. Davie got his rifle out of the truck and fired the gun in the air. The bear ran off.

The Park Ranger heard the shot. His office was near to them. He drove his truck to their location to see what was happening.

The bear had scared Jenny. She told the Park Ranger she did not like big bears and feared the bear would hurt her mama. The Ranger told her, "Bears seldom come into the park. They keep back in the woods most of the time. He also warned to not leave food outside where the bear could smell the food."

Jenny had crawled up in her mother's lap, and Jennifer could see how frightened she was. She wondered if camping - was going to be the right adventure for her precious little girl. Jennifer took her back inside the camper, and she sat and held Jenny in her arms.

Jenny said, "Mom, I was scared that big bear would hurt you. That bad guy had hurt you, and I did not want that big ole bear to hurt you. I do not like "Big Brown Teddy Bears." I take all the teddy bears out of my room when I get home.

When I see them, I will think about the bear I thought would hurt you. I love you, Mama, and I do not want you hurt again."

Jennifer, "Held her daughter tighter and said, "Jenny, you are so precious and dear to me. I am so sorry that the bear scared you so bad and you feared it would hurt me.

I am sorry, too, that I had been hurt, and it took me a little while to heal. I am feeling better and getting stronger every day. Thanks, precious, for your love and telling me the bear was behind me.

I missed precious time with each of you when I was hurting so bad and no one could touch or hug me. I feel safe now with the bad guy in prison where he can never hurt me or anyone again."

Davie and Jimmy had gone back to the lake to retrieve their fishing gear. They had caught several and decided to cook them over an open fire and have fish for supper.

The fish tasted great. Jennifer got some pork, beans, and things that would taste good with the fish. They enjoyed the fresh air and the great-tasting fish cooked outside.

There was a picnic table near their camper.

Everyone helped to clean up the cooking vessels. They put away the food in a cooler in the truck.

Jennifer was tired. She was better but not back to where she needed to be yet. It was getting late, and she was ready to go inside the camper for the night.

Davie and Jimmy agreed with Jennifer it was bedtime. Jenny had fallen asleep in her mother's arms. Davie had gently lifted her and put her in her bunk bed. She never woke up, and he covered her with a light blanket.

Jimmy had already climbed up and got in his bunk bed.

Davie and Jennifer turned back the covers. They pulled the curtain so they could get ready for bed. When Jennifer was in bed, Davie pushed the curtains back to see the kids in their beds.

Later in the night, the sounds of Jenny crying and screaming woke them all up. Jimmy had already climbed down from his bunk and held her, telling her she was safe.

Davie and Jennifer slipped her from her bed. Jennifer held her and spoke softly, assuring her they were all safe.

Jimmy said, "Dad, Mom, she was screaming because she thought the bear would hurt you. The bear scared her a lot."

Jenny reached out to her dad. He took her in his arms and told her he loved her.

He said, "Jenny, Daddy is so sorry that big old bear scared you. We did not know there were any bears anywhere close to this park. I will make sure that bear never bothers you again."

Jennifer put Jenny in her bed, and Davie spent the night in Jenny's bed. Holding her in her arms, Jenny had gone to sleep. Jennifer removed her arms and was finally able to go to sleep.

The next morning, they gathered around the table in the camper. Davie did not like knowing a bear was roaming in those woods, which might harm his loved ones.

Davie said, "We came here to have fun, fish, and enjoy being here at this park. I am ready for us to load up and go somewhere else where we can feel safe.

I would have never come here if I had known any bears anywhere in this part of the state or their parks. Daddy is so sorry, Jenny, that you were frightened so badly by this big brown bear."

Jenny said, "I am sorry, Daddy, that the bear scared me. We were having fun, and I liked it here. I do not want to leave here. I hope the bear never comes back."

Jennifer said, "Davie, their safety is important. I think we can make some calls and find another area to camp where we can have fun, and there are no bears in that area."

Davie said, "I will talk to the Ranger and let him know we plan to leave. I will ask him if he knows of some other state park with no bears in that area."

Jennifer started getting things packed away and secured so they could leave the camp. Jenny helped her some.

Jimmy was putting the fishing gears in the truck and helping his mom load up things from the camper and take them to the truck.

Davie returned and said, "The Park Ranger is sorry we are leaving but understands why. He suggested a state park close to this area, where there had never been any bears in their park.

They all wanted to camp out, so they hooked the camper to the truck and headed to the other state park.

When they arrived, they noticed the area they would be staying in was not heavily wooded, and the Park Ranger told them he had never seen any bears in that area of the state or their park.

They loved the state park. It was a better park. There was an area where they had swings and slides and a place to swim, bike trails, and lots of things to do while camping there.

The trailers were parked further apart, so they had plenty of room for camping.

They checked into the park, got their camper set up again, and were ready to do more camping.

The camp facilities were easy to walk to from their trailer. They even had a place where they served hamburgers and hot dogs.

Jennifer loved this camp. It was a much better place for children.

During their week there, they had a lot of fun. They sat around their campfire at night, talked, sang funny songs, and laughed. Everyone had a wonderful time and never saw a bear at that park.

On their last night there, they ordered hamburgers and hot dogs from the camp café and returned them to their trailer. Jennifer told Davie they needed to camp there again soon.

She felt more relaxed and rested than she had since Rick had raped her. Her body was healing, and she had more energy now.

They got everything packed up and loaded. The truck was hooked up to the camper, and they headed home. This park was not as close as the other one, but the perfect one for them as a family.

They arrived home late that evening, tired and worn out, but they wanted to return and camp out again at that park.

The next morning, Davie and their family took the camper back over to the farm to store it in the shed.

The kids were eager to tell their grandparents all about their adventures camping. Jenny told them about the bear scaring her in the first place. They went camping and had to find somewhere else to camp.

Irene sat there listening to her great-grandchildren's fun they were having.

She was so glad they all lived nearby to be together more often. She only wished Charlie could have stayed with them longer and got to share in these activities.

She knew God knew it was the right time for him to go to heaven. One of these days, she would join him, but right now, she thanked God for the love and care her family gave her.

Selling this house to Tom and Peggy had worked out great. She and Peggy had always gotten along great. They enjoyed time together.

Building the bedroom and bathroom was a wise investment for them. She felt so secure being here with them.

Davie was grateful Tom and Peggy shared their camper with them. Tom helped him check it out at the shed and ensured everything was okay and could be stored there.

Davie, Jennifer, and the kids enjoyed lunch with them.

After leaving, they drove down to his mom and dad's place. It was nice his mom and dad lived next door to her mom and dad.

Jerry and Marilyn were glad to see them and hear all the exciting stories from them about their camping trip.

Jenny made sure they knew about the bear. She had not mentioned it until they got back home.

Jimmy was full of stories of things he did with his dad and with the family. He told them it was a wonderful place for kids to go camping.

Jerry and Davie spent time talking about the camping trip and things he and Jennifer enjoyed doing. Jerry was glad to see his son so relaxed, and Jennifer was more at peace and relaxed. Going camping was good for all of them.

Marilyn and Jennifer had stepped out back to her special garden gazebo. The kids were outside playing.

Marilyn said, "Jennifer, this trip was a healing adventure for you. I am glad the four of you could get away. You have all been through so much lately, and it was time for you to have fun."

Marilyn had taken teacups and some tea with them when they went outside. She poured them some tea.

Jennifer sat there sipping her tea. Marilyn always got the best-flavored teas. Neither one spoke for a while.

Jennifer said, "I am eager to get on with my life. Davie has been patient with me and kind and caring. I have not been able to express my love to him physically since the rape occurred.

I was a mess inside because of Rick's brutality when he raped me. I am slowly healing, and hopefully, I will soon be healed.

Davie is so understanding, but I miss our beautiful ways of expressing our love to each other. It scares me to think I might not be able, even after healing, to express myself completely due to damage done to me internally."

Marilyn said, "Jennifer, I am so proud of Davie and his caring, patient, kind, and understanding.

He will wait forever if needed and would understand if you could not express love physically. There are many ways of saying I love you and showing it.

Leave it in God's hands. He will help you to find ways to continue to express your feelings and do so while you are healing.

When they returned home, Jennifer started some laundry and started down the hallway. She saw a bag in the hallway. It was outside Jenny's room. She wanted to get rid of teddy bears so they would not remind her of the big bear in the woods. Jennifer took the bag and stored it in the closet in her room.

Weeks went by since their vacation. Jennifer found herself with some renewed energy. It was great feeling good again.

The therapist told Jennifer she was doing good and just made appointments as she felt she needed a therapist. She told Jennifer how proud she was of her accomplishments in her therapy.

Jennifer and Davie loved their church and church family. The kids loved their Sunday school teachers.

The church had planned a hayride for Davie and Jennifer's Sunday School class. Everyone was looking forward to this get-to-get-together hayride.

One of the church members had a horse, wagon, and quite a few acres, perfect for this outing.

Jennifer arranged for Jimmy and Jenny to spend the night with their Grandpa Tom and Grandma Peggy on Saturday night of the hayride.

Jennifer's mom and dad also attended the church where they attended. This was the same church Tom had attended with his mom and dad as a boy.

They would take the kids to church the next morning.

Grandma Irene was also able to go to church with them. She loved being back in church and hoped her health would make it possible to attend every Sunday.

Saturday night, the class met at Bro. James house. He had the hay in the wagon and the horse hooked up to the wagon when they arrived.

His wife made sure sandwiches and other picnic food items were available for them to enjoy. There were also some cookies and other sweet treats for them.

They met early enough Saturday to enjoy the hayride before it got dark. Bro. James had hooked up some lanterns in case it got dark before they returned to the house.

The pastor stood up in the wagon before they took off on the hayride. He said, "I am thrilled to be the pastor of our church.

Your faithfulness in attendance to church has been great, and your willingness to teach and help promote the work of the Lord in whatever ways you can has been inspirational in so many ways.

I want to encourage you to continue to reach out to others outside of our church family and do so by encouraging others to seek God's will for them in their lives.

Invite them to our church if they do not have a church they attend. If they do not know God as their Savior, share the plan of salvation with them: I have several things to mention to you that will be helpful.

A. They need to recognize they are sinners and need forgiveness for their sins.

B. Ask God to forgive them of their sins.

C. Allow God to enter their hearts and give them that peace that comes from being a child of God.

D. Help them realize that a meaningful change occurs in their hearts when they are a child of God."

The pastor said, "Time for a hayride, and he sat down with his wife and enjoyed the hayride with some wonderful church family members."

Davie and Jennifer loved being with this group and sharing these moments with other brothers and sisters in Christ.

Everyone was enjoying the hayride and the smell of fresh hay and being together. Some sang a sing-along, like "Over the Mountains and Through the Woods."

They knew it might be cool in the evening hours, so those who came brought blankets to use during the hayride.

Everyone had fun and returned before the sun set over the mountains.

Hot chocolate, coffee, and other drinks were there for them and food to eat when they got off the wagon. It was a great evening; everyone looked forward to more events together.

Tom, Peggy, and Irene sat at the table the following Monday after the grandkids spent Saturday night with them.

Tom said, "Peggy and Mom, our decision to move back here was good. I know what I am about to say. I have said several times, but I am so glad we could move back here and buy this house.

Mama, we are glad you are here with us in your home. The great-grandkids sure enjoyed being here with you, Mom. They are good kids and a joy to have in our home."

The phone rang, and Peggy answered it. It was Bobby and Eve calling them.

Bobby said, "Mom, I called to let you know we are taking a few days off from work and want to come up this weekend and stay several days if that works okay with you.

We want to spend time with Davie, Jennifer, and the kids on Saturday for a gathering at your place, Mom. Looking forward to time with both of you and grandma."

Peggy said, "I am so glad you are getting some time off from work, and we would love to have you both here for some time together as a family.

I know your grandma will be excited knowing you are coming. She always loved it when you and Jennifer came to visit with them.

She never says much about Charlie being gone, but I see it in her eyes, the sadness and how much she misses him.

I am glad we bought the home place so she will always have a home here in her home with us. We both get along great, and she is a joy to be with."

Bobby told her they would be up there late Friday evening, and he would call Jennifer and let them know they were coming up for a visit.

After she hung up the phone, she got a cup of coffee and sat on the porch. Looking around her, she felt such peace being there. Charlie had built this home for his family.

Peggy said, "I am glad we could buy this house. We love being able to help with the care and upkeep of this house. I know you would not have been able, Irene, to do all the work here without Charlie."

Irene said, "Peggy, I am so glad you are happy here and love this home. I am also thankful that when I leave here and go to heaven, you will be here to continue caring for the home."

The door opened, and Tom joined her with his coffee. He sat down beside her. They sat together, enjoying life here in this home and this town.

Tom said, "Living in Rosewood all those years was great, but now that I am retired, I can be here to help Mom. I sure love being back home.

God had a hand in all this working out the way it did. You and Mom seem to have so much fun doing things together. I am blessed now with two good cooks."

Peggy sat her empty cup down and snuggled up closer to Tom. They had enjoyed some good years together.

Irene had gone back inside. Both sat silently, listening to the birds singing in the nearby tree.

Hearing a loud crash, they jumped up and ran inside. They found Irene grinning from ear to ear. She looked up at them and said, "I am fine. I just knocked off this silly lamp."

Wiping a few tears, she said, "I miss Charlie, but I will not miss that lamp. I wouldn't say I liked that silly-looking lamp, but Charlie really liked it and had bought it, moved my lamp off the table, and put it on that table.

Well, it is only fitting that the lamp is gone since he is gone now. He got to enjoy it all those years. I never did like that lamp.

I had not planned to move it but was not watching closely enough and bumped into that silly lamp."

Tom grinned, got the broom and dustpan, and cleaned up the mess from the broken lamp. He remembered his dad buying that lamp at an auction they had gone to that day.

It was a farm auction, and his dad bought the old wagon and a few other tools still in his garage.

They had sold some of the furniture in the old farmhouse. Her husband had died. She was selling everything and moving in with her daughter.

Friday evening, Bobby and Eve drove up to Linkersville. They were excited about being there for a few days and eager to share some good news with everyone.

Saturday morning, Bobby woke up to the smell of coffee.

Eve was still sleeping, so he made his way downstairs. He found his mom and grandma in the kitchen.

His mom put some coffee on the table for him, and his grandma sat down with her coffee.

Grandma Irene said, "Grandson, you have always been such a joy.

I know your mom and dad adopted you when you were a baby, but to me, you were my grandbaby in every way. I never thought of you as being adopted, but instead thought of you as a special gift to us from God.

I love you, and I love your sweet, beautiful wife."

Eve had awakened and headed downstairs.

She heard her name and Grandma Irene's words a few minutes before.

She hugged Bobby, and then she hugged Grandma Irene.

She said, "Thank you for loving me too. I love you also, and you are such an inspiration and joy for all of us.

Bobby has shared many stories from the time spent here with you and his grandpa. This is a perfect place for the family to gather for visits."

Grandma Irene wiped a few tears and hugged Eve and Bobby. Leaving them to enjoy their coffee, she returned to the kitchen.

She thanked God for all her blessings and the joys of the family being here.

Peggy returned from taking coffee to Tom out in the garage. He was busy with a wood project in the garage.

He loved working outside. He had found some things stored in the upper part of the garage. He had been going through the things to see what he wanted to keep and what he wanted to get rid of.

Tom heard a truck coming down the driveway, and it was Davie, Jennifer, and those precious grandkids. Everyone inside the house heard the truck pull up and walked out on the porch. Jenny and Jimmy came running to them. Everyone got hugs from the grandkids. Tom had come to the house.

Eve, Peggy, and Jennifer helped Grandma Irene put all the food on the table for breakfast.

Jenny wanted to put the fork, knife, and spoon on the plates, so she got to help them get those things on the table and ready for breakfast.

After breakfast and the kitchen was cleaned, the women joined Tom, Bobby, and Davie on the porch.

Jimmy and Jenny were outside enjoying some games.

Eve had joined Bobby on the swing. It was a large screened-in porch, so they could find places to sit and enjoy a cool breeze.

Bobby said, "Since we are all together now and have eaten a wonderful breakfast, I think this is a suitable time to talk to you about something that involves all of us."

Tom looked over at Peggy, and she had a look of concern on her face. Tom feared his son had been offered a job elsewhere and would be moving. Surely not, though; they had just moved into a home he grew up in.

Bobby and Eve were grinning and stood up. Bobby said, "We wanted to come here and tell you our plans.

This involves you too, so it is a joy to share this news with you today."

Eve said, "Yes, you are the first to know that the doctor said, "I am pregnant, and we are going to have a baby."

Everyone was on their feet and giving Bobby and Eve hugs. They were so excited and so happy for them.

Jennifer was in tears. She was thrilled to know Bobby and Eve would have a baby and yet sad that the baby girl she lost would not be here to enjoy growing up with her cousin.

Jennifer hugged them and told them she was thrilled and knew they would be wonderful parents for this baby they were expecting.

Bobby knew his sister and had always been there for her all those years, and he had seen that happy but sad look in her eyes.

He hugged her and said, "Sis, I am thrilled I will be a father. I thought of the baby you recently lost.

I wish your baby could have been here to enjoy growing up with our baby.

You will be someone Eve can turn to, like a sister, to help her during this pregnancy. She is scared and excited that she is pregnant. Her doctor had told her years ago she would never be able to have any children.

She was reluctant to marry me because she knew she had been told she would never get pregnant. I assured her that if she never had children, we would enjoy the children in our family. We are thrilled though she is pregnant."

Jennifer said, "Thanks for sharing that with me, and I will be there for her and you. I look forward to Eve and me going shopping and buying baby stuff.

I might even have some trivial things I had bought for a baby girl if she sees she is having a girl. It will be nice having a baby to hold again in my arms. I love you both and am thrilled at the news of the baby."

Tom said, "This grandfather would like a few moments to speak." Everyone sat back down.

Tom said, "I am thrilled we are adding a little one to this family. I welcome this baby into our lives and our hearts.

I was going through stuff in the attic and found something I did not have the heart to eliminate. I wanted to keep one of the things I found in the garage. I have cleaned and polished it and wanted to show you what a treasure I found."

They all got up and followed Tom to the garage.

Sitting on the garage floor was the most beautiful, crafted baby cradle. It was in excellent shape.

Grandma Irene walked over to the cradle and, with tears in her eyes, said, "Charlie never told me he saved that baby cradle.

He made that for our baby. We were married for a couple of years, and I got pregnant. I lost my first baby at four months of pregnancy.

I was so upset and brokenhearted. Like Jennifer, I grieved the loss of that baby and could not bear to even look at that cradle.

Charlie took the cradle, and I never knew what he did with it. Now, we have a great-grandbaby who can be rocked in that cradle. I will love spending time with the baby and rocking and holding it. God has given you a baby to give birth to, Eve, and the two of you to care for the rest of your lives.

I am thankful God has allowed me to be here to share in this blessing. Wish Charlie was here to share this baby cradle with us. Charlie made this cradle himself, so Bobby and Eve, you are getting something made by your grandfather for your baby.

Charlie was a good carpenter and made a lot of beautiful things for our home.

I know why Charlie never told me about saving this cradle. He saw how I grieved the loss of my first child and never even mentioned it when I got pregnant with you, Tom, and your brother.

Time helps to heal old wounds, and I can say today that I am thankful Charlie saved this cradle, and with joy in my heart, thank you, Tom, for finding it and making it possible for them to use. Use it with my love and blessings."

She hugged them both, walked over to the cradle, ran her hands over the smooth wood, looked up with a smile, and said, "This cradle is perfect for your baby."

Eve hugged her and said, "It will be used and kept forever."

Jennifer and Davie were thrilled to hear the good news about Bobby and Eve expecting a baby. They knew Bobby and Eve would care for their baby with such devotion.

When the weekend ended and Bobby and Eve went home, Jennifer sat alone on the porch. Davie had gone to work, and her parents had insisted that the kids stay a few more days.

Sitting alone on the porch with her coffee, she felt the tears coming into her eyes. She blinked and wiped her eyes.

Why was she crying? She was so happy about her brother and Eve announcing they would have a baby. The more she thought about their shared great news, the sadder she became.

Returning to the kitchen, she refilled her cup with coffee and returned to the porch. Hearing a car coming down the road, she suddenly panicked and thought of Rick coming down the road.

She knew he was locked up in prison, but she remembered vividly the time Rick came down to their house, and he raped her, causing her to nearly lose her own life and her losing her baby.

The tears kept coming so fast, realizing that her baby was gone to be with God because of Rick. She would never hold her and be able to raise and care for or see her until she died and would be in heaven with her baby and grandpa.

She never even saw her after birth because she had slipped into unconsciousness.

She was crying so hard and filled with sorrow that she never knew when the car pulled up in front of the house.

Davie saw her on the porch and could hear her crying and sobbing when he exited the car. Rushing upon the porch, he said, "Sweetheart, it is me, Davie. I am here for you."

Davie knew Jennifer had never really broken down and cried like she was crying today because of the death of their baby girl.

He was unsure what had stirred such emotions but figured it might be her brother and his wife announcing they would have a baby.

He whispered in her ear, "Go ahead and cry, Jennifer."

Suddenly, Jennifer realized someone was holding her. She started screaming and pushing him away.

He kept talking to her, and she realized then it was Davie. The tears blinded her to who was holding her, but his voice and the gentle way he kept holding her helped her to realize it was someone who loved her and was there for her.

The tears finally stopped. Davie shed some tears, too, as he held his beloved, precious wife in his arms. Therapy had helped her, but she had refused to allow her mind to accept the loss of the baby.

It had been too painful after the rape for her to even think about not only losing her baby but being told she could never have children again due to the damage done to her by the brutal rape.

Lifting Jennifer from the chair on the porch, he wrapped his arms around her, hugged her, and they went inside.

I will always remember my baby girl, and we will never forget her. Thank you for caring for her burial when I was unconscious in the hospital.

I want to go to the cemetery today, take some flowers, and put them on her grave. Those flowers will be our way of saying we love you and will never forget you. I wish I could have seen the baby before it was buried. I will never know what it looked like.

Davie pulled a picture out of his wallet and said, "Jennifer, I was able to see her in the hospital, and I took a picture of her. I have been saving this picture to show you when it was the right time."

He handed the picture to her. She looked at her baby Janie Irene and smiled.

She said, "Davie, she is the perfect likeness to me when I was a baby. She is so pretty. I will treasure this photo always. Thank you for getting us a picture of our daughter.

Walking hand in hand, they walked to the car. On their way to the cemetery, they stopped to purchase a stuffed teddy bear and to get some flowers to put on the grave.

Arriving at the cemetery, Davie stopped the car and turned to Jennifer. Looking into her eyes, he saw her pain but knew this was something she needed to do today.

He said, "Jennifer, I am here for you, and we will never forget our baby girl. I also feel the pain of our loss, so we will comfort each other and let God help and care for us during this time of our loss.

I came home early today because I needed to take some time off. I am glad I can be here for you at this time."

They got out of the car, and Jennifer stopped. Looking up at Davie, she saw his pain and was so grateful God had blessed her with a companion and husband like Davie.

She said, "Davie, your love, that of the family, friends, and God helped me to make it after the rape and loss of our baby.

Without that support, I might not be here. Thank you so much, Davie, for your love and understanding."

They placed the flowers and a Teddy bear on the grave, left in tears, and returned to the car. She looked back at the grave and knew she would return there again to show her love for her precious baby. She also knew her baby was in God's hands and being cared for by the angels.

When they returned home, Jennifer said, "My therapist told me the day would come when the complete realization of losing my baby would come. I would cry like I had not cried this whole time.

The therapist knew I was unwilling to accept it completely. I'm so glad you came home and were able to be here for me today.

Hearing the news about my little niece or nephew was great news but a reminder of the loss of my baby.

I also heard a car coming down the driveway this morning while sitting on the porch. It suddenly started bringing back the day Rick came down the driveway and forcibly shoved me into the house, and raped me.

I never knew when you drove up to the house. I only became aware of it being you, not Rick, when I kept hearing your voice, those words of love, and the gentle way you held me. Davie, I am ready now to move on completely with life.

I will never forget the past, but I will move on with life and be thankful for having you and our children and loved ones here with us.

So glad we are attending church, have a wonderful pastor and church family, and have God in our lives."

Davie suggested they go for a drive through the mountains. He knew a beautiful spot where you could look down at the valley from the top of that mountain.

He found the place and pulled the car over. They got out of the car, and Jennifer was filled with joy in looking down into the valley and knowing where they were now was up on top of the mountains.

She knew each had been in the valley with all its sorrows, anguish, and pain, but now they were standing atop the mountain.

They both knew there would be other valleys in life but were grateful to see where they had come from and where they are now at this time in their life.

Smiling, they left the mountains and were ready to face life's next adventures. They knew, with time and healing, that joy was there for them in the future. The kids would be in school soon, bringing new adventures and joy, watching their children grow up to become adults.

God is love, joy, and happiness, and there for them throughout their life. Because they were saved, they would someday see their baby and grandparents and those they love waiting for them in heaven.

Davie looked over at Jennifer as he was driving home, and he saw that a feeling of peace had come over her, and she smiled.

Jennifer looked at Davie and said, "Let us go home and get busy living again.

I love you so much, and I am eager to get completely physically healed so I can be there for you and our children in special ways."

Dropping her head, she said, "Thank you, Lord, for our blessings and two precious children we can raise and care for. Thank you for our baby girl, and know we will be with her again someday. Amen

With the picture in her hand, they went inside the house. She found a frame she had bought for the baby's first picture. They framed it and treasured having her forever in their hearts.

They heard Jimmy and Jenny laughing outside over what her grandpa said when he brought them home. It was sweet music to their ears.

Tom stepped inside the door and told the kids he loved them and would see them soon.

He left, and Jenny and Jimmy came inside.

Jenny saw the photo and said, "Mom, is that a picture of our baby?"

Jimmy looked at it and smiled.

Jenny said, "I think she looks like you and me. Mama, she is a beautiful baby sister. Dad, I am glad you got us a picture of our baby sister."

Jennifer decided she would have an 8 x 10 picture made of Janie Irene soon. She was indeed a beautiful baby.

They were smiling when they looked at their baby sister in the photo on the table.

Everyone decided to walk down to the lake and stood there for a while. The sun was setting, and a beautiful glow was across the lake. This was a beautiful place, and their home was a special place for all of them.

The four of them stood there together with their arms around each other. They knew God was there with them as they gazed across the water and enjoyed the sunset.